Also by Lynne Markham

Lynne Markham

BLAZING STAR

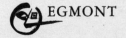 EGMONT

For Dr Sue

Acknowlegdements
I would like to thank the Mansfield and Sutton
Astronomical Society for their help and advice. I would also
like to thank Mrs Sandra Cockburn and the Brisan School of Dancing
for their amazing tolerance!

First published in Great Britain in 2002
by Egmont Books Ltd
239 Kensington High Street, London W8 6SA

ISBN 0 7497 4625 4

10 9 8 7 6 5 4 3 2 1

A CIP catalogue record for this book is available
from the British Library.

Typeset by Avon DataSet Ltd, Bidford on Avon B50 4JH
Printed and bound in Great Britain by
Cox & Wyman Ltd, Reading, Berkshire

Contents

Author's Note

I am aware that there is a great deal of discussion on the correct terminology to use for the Native American.

This latter term is the one which is most preferred. However, a boy living in a British inner-city would, I believe, more naturally refer to Indians. In using indian with a lower case i, my intention is to cause as little offence as possible to the Native American people.

The Star

You can see a lot of stars in autumn. There's Saturn, like a tiny light glowing. And there's Venus and Jupiter. Jupiter's small and bright like a torch being switched on and off. I was in the Observatory with my mate Brian and his wife Maureen and some of the others, when Brian said to me, 'Come and look at this, Geoffrey, he's bright tonight. You'll never see Jupiter better than that. There'll be a frost later, I shouldn't wonder.'

I put my eye to the telescope and was looking at Jupiter. You almost couldn't look without hurting your eyes. I blinked and looked again and the brilliance grew even whiter and began to whirl, slowly at first, and then faster and faster like a Catherine Wheel. In the middle of the whirl this eye appeared that was redder than fire and redder than blood. It was so fiery you could hear it crackle and hiss with the heat and the hissing was like millions of sparks flying out in a blazing shower.

It wasn't Jupiter. It wasn't a star I'd seen before. It wasn't a star anyone else could see. Looking at it made my face go stiff and tears start up at the back of my eyes. Stupidly, I put a hand out. I think I wanted to touch the star, or to fly with it, or to *be* the star, but it was light years away from me. Maybe that was why I wanted to cry.

'All right, Geoffrey?' Brian came up and put a hand on my arm.

In a second the whirling stopped altogether, the red eye disappeared and Jupiter was back, just clear and glittering in the black night sky.

I shrugged him off. 'I'm OK,' I said.

I got down from the platform where the telescope was and hunched up inside my coat. At the back of my head the blazing star still fizzed like a light that's never been really put out.

The Omen

If it hadn't been for Ivy stepping on Gran's bad toe I might have stayed Geoffrey Parker for ever and never become a Geoff. But that was after a lot of other ifs: if Mum and Dad hadn't gone to Africa; if I hadn't gone to live with Gran; if Gran hadn't gone dancing that Wednesday afternoon. All those ifs led up to Blazing Star like a trail for me to find.

I got in from school and Gran was sitting in the kitchen with one leg crossed over the other, rubbing her toe.

'It's me corn,' she said with her face all creased. You could see the beginning of her long winter knickers where her flowery skirt had got pushed up. 'Smack on to it she went with her best gold shoe. She forgot she was the man, you see. And pain! I've never felt pain like it. Be a good lad and run to the chemist's for a corn plaster. Then when you get back we'll have our tea.'

I picked some money off the table and went out. I heard

the click of the radio behind me and some music come on, and even though the music was gross the tightness that was in my chest settled down again. Gran's not going to die today, I thought, I won't be left all on my own.

Outside it was still daylight. I thought I could see Betelgeuse like a small red eye in the sky. It might just have been something on my glasses but afterwards I reckoned it was a kind of omen. First the blazing star and then Betelgeuse, the reddest star in the sky, shining like it was put there just for me.

I went down our road and took a short cut through the twitchel to the main road and Boots. Boots was busy with little kids and mums buying bottles of cough medicine, but Jean, who serves, said, 'Hiya, Geoffrey. Gran OK?'

'She wants a corn plaster,' I said. And went red like when I have to ask for sennacots on days when Gran's tubes start playing up. A lady next to me giggled a bit.

'Ivy step on her toe again? She'll have to find a bloke, Geoffrey, then she won't always have to be the man.' Jean and the lady giggled together, then Jean gave me the plasters in a plastic bag.

I went marching off down Hockley which was the longer route back home. In a minute the shops had fizzled out and factories began to line the road. You could hear the clack of knitting machines and now and then a voice shouting out. I wasn't bothering to look where I went, I wasn't even thinking much, just replaying 'Jupiter' from *The Planets* Suite inside my head and maybe humming bits out loud.

Then I turned a corner and the indian brave was there.

Smack on the pavement in front of me.

Perhaps it was the setting sun that did it, but he seemed enormous, ten feet tall. And his body blazed fiercely, red and gold. A spear was clutched in his right hand. His eyes gleamed red with the sun behind them and his hair was like a blood-red stream. There were three tall feathers at the back of his head and his clothes were painted with moons and stars.

I stopped bang in my tracks with the corn plasters still clutched in my hand. Then I stared at the indian, at his flaming eyes. At the red stripes running across his face and the necklace made out of sharp white claws. And while I looked this stuff came off him. Not a thing you could smell or touch. It was more like a kind of force that made me think I was looking at a past or a future I'd never seen before. I recognised something but didn't know what.

The hairs on the back of my neck went up.

And the indian glared back as if he knew me, Geoffrey Parker who lived with his gran and wore specs glued up with sellotape and lumpy jumpers she knitted for him.

I looked at him and I felt like yelling, only not with fear, but with a kind of awe and a longing for something I wasn't sure of.

And then the sun dropped out of sight. The flames round the indian slowly died down, and I did a stupid Geoffrey thing: I turned round fast and ran back home.

Magic Eyes

I'm always scared Gran's going to die. If she has a pain or her indigestion (Gran can't eat cabbage or celery) or palpitations like she sometimes has, I think: that's it, she'll die. I almost daren't go to bed sometimes in case I wake up and find her dead. It's like there's a great scary chunk of something missing in my life, and it's people. Since Mum and Dad went to Africa there's just me and Gran and some cousins we hate. So if Gran pops off, that's it.

When Mum and Dad went Gran said, 'Well now, there's just you and me, Geoffrey. We'll have to make the best of it.'

Gran's full of sayings like that. 'You have to keep active, don't you?' Or, 'Worrying never helped anyone.'

Mum and Dad went suddenly. They'd always wanted to go to Africa. They talked about it and looked at pictures. They wanted to go and dig up the desert looking for long-dead people and stuff. And one day they really upped and went.

'Why didn't they take me?' I asked. I was crying, actually, with my head on Gran's knee.

And Gran didn't answer for a while. She stroked my hair and I could smell mothballs and onions coming off her dress. Then she said, 'Sometimes you can't always do what you want. They're happy where they are, Geoffrey my duck. And you'll be happy one day, you'll see.'

So I waited for a letter but it didn't come. Maybe they were too far away from a postbox. Or maybe they were just so happy and pleased with what they were doing that they didn't really need me any more. Maybe the best news I could have of them was the pictures I made inside my head.

Sunshine. Monkeys. A great roaring moon. I pictured the Southern Cross as well with Centaurus in the middle. I wondered if they were really seeing what I was just picturing. Centaurus. A great winged star in the sky light years away.

Sometimes I wrote letters. I never posted them. If they don't write to me, I won't write to them. Why should I care anyway? They just wandered off wearing stupid hats to dig up mouldy bones and jugs.

So like I said, there's just Gran and me.

That morning I woke up thinking about the indian. It's like he saw me, and he knew me better after ten seconds of looking than I knew myself. It's like he was that powerful and that fantastic he would be in my dreams for a long time to come.

At breakfast Gran said her toe still hurt. She looked even older without her teeth and I worried again.

'Good job it's bingo today,' she said. 'I won't be on my pins so much. Now Geoffrey, you eat that egg. It'll make you into a big strong lad.'

Gran was wearing slippers with a slit cut out to ease her bad toe. She'd a single pink curler stuck in her hair.

'Bingo's gambling,' I said, primly. 'It's completely mindless. It's the last resort of the total brain-dead.'

And Gran stopped in the middle of pouring the tea. She's a face that's soft and pink and loose, like ice-cream starting to melt away. You wouldn't think a face like that could look at me the way Gran did then. Sharp and measuring. A Bible look.

'You've a lot to learn, my lad,' she said.

I ate my breakfast and went outside and dawdled more than I usually did so I was late for school. I had to go to reception. WELCOME stares at you in big red letters running down the wall. Next to that a notice says:

Be polite to receptionist
Sign at reception on late sheet
Have sheet countersigned by member of SMT
Collect white slip and have it signed
Give slip to teacher in class

A group of kids were sitting on chairs waiting to see the Head. 'Hey-up, Geoffrey,' said one of them. Another one shot me a look like a bullet and said very quietly, 'Freak!'

I did the slip thing and went into class and nobody even noticed me. Miss Turner was talking to some girls and some kids were fast asleep at their desks. I took my coat off and sat myself down and didn't even try to do any work because there was nothing to do and no point anyway. They don't try to teach you very much here, all they want is for you to keep quiet.

So I thought about the indian again. And about Betelgeuse seeming to point the way. Just looking at the indian made me feel different. Like a crack was opening up in my imagination. So instead of just seeing the same old Geoffrey I was seeing someone else who was bigger and braver and stronger than me.

Then the desk behind me got tipped up and smashed down on the back of my chair. I gave a yelp and Miss Turner looked over, I saw her think something and change her mind and Michelle behind me said, 'Miss, I want you. Come over here.'

People always do what Michelle says, even though she's so small and thin. She just fixes you with her mocking eyes and gives out these weird, secret smiles.

Miss Turner came over and she'd some stuff in her hand. 'These are adverts,' she said, dishing them out. 'You've to check them for adjectives and puns and so on. Who is the target audience? Try to rewrite it for someone else. You're to tell me all about it next week. I'll be going round the class and you'll be speaking out loud, so make sure you've done the work properly.'

Michelle's advert had a mobile phone on it, and Sharon's had a girl with big shiny lips. I covered my advert up with my arm. There was a picture of a man in carpet slippers doing a stupid Hawaiian dance. The writing said, 'Grow old disgracefully. Drink PRUNE JUICE.'

I reckon Miss Turner gave me that advert on purpose on account of me being what Gran calls a young fogey. She means someone who doesn't care about pop groups but knows all about Mozart and the stars.

In a corner a fight was breaking out and Darren was bashing away at the computer pretending it was some kind of honky-tonk piano. He was miming words and rolling his eyes and the stupid thing wasn't even plugged in.

Miss Turner looked at the kids who were fast asleep and said, 'It's good to see you can work on your own.' Then she shuffled all her papers together and coughed and said to us in a false-bright voice, 'Right now! Don't forget your adverts next week.'

The rest of the day went on like that and some kids went missing in the afternoon, but I stuck it out until home time when I meant to go back to Gran's. But I didn't.

I went to see the indian again, even though he was probably just a trick of light and not real at all. I went to Hockley Lane where I'd seen him before, but he wasn't there.

I was going to go back towards Gran's house, but a sudden pain in my guts made me stay where I was, doubled up. It was the same pain I got when Mum and Dad went away, coming out of nowhere. When I stood up again I heard the music in the factory change from *Lady in Red* to *Starry, Starry Night*. At the same time I saw the factory's name in red and white letters lit up over the windows. STAR KNITWEAR. The A's were like little red stars, flaming.

Suddenly the music stopped. It was so quiet I could hear my feet going to the factory door. The door was set back down a passageway and on the wall of the passage there was another star with a deep red centre and a trail of silver sparks behind it.

It was the star I'd seen instead of Jupiter. While I looked I could hear it start to crackle and fizz and my head felt weird, like it was whirling round.

I closed my eyes. And when I opened them again I was somewhere else. I was in a meadow that was broad and green, and so bright that the sunshine made me blind.

I squinted and put my school bag down on the grass. The air was so clear and fresh and sparkling you felt you could drink it. Birds were shouting from the high blue sky and even the grass was singing.

In front of me there was a boy about my age, or maybe a little younger. He was thin and brown and wore nothing except for a cloth fastened round his waist. His hair was shiny and hung to his shoulders and when he saw me he waved as if I was already his friend.

'Watch me shoot this arrow,' he said. 'Watch me, my friend, I shoot to win!'

He took an arrow from the quiver on his back and flexed it against the bow. Then he shot the arrow and it soared in an arc and landed close to another arrow roughly fifty metres away. He jumped up and down and some other boys laughed and jostled him. He called again, 'Come closer to me, Magic Eyes! See what luck you bring me today!'

I picked my bag up and went a bit closer feeling stupid and clumsy and overdressed. But the boy just laughed and showed his teeth. 'Watch!' he said to me again. 'None of the others can shoot as far!'

He was right. When the last arrow was shot a great shout went up, 'Long Horn wins again today!'

With a high, clear laugh Long Horn took my arm and swooped me across the grass with him. 'Ten arrows I have won today and tomorrow I may win ten more!' He was pulling arrows out of the ground and I was pulling them with him as fast as I could and sticking them into the quiver again. The other kids were milling around, jostling him and laughing and slapping his back. They couldn't see me. It was almost like I was a part of Long Horn.

'Magic Eyes. You're with me now.'

Long Horn said that with his arm around my shoulders and I could feel his body like taut, hard wire.

'But I don't know you,' I said, stupidly.

And Long Horn went very still. He stared at me as if he was looking into something I couldn't see; a care he was carrying secretly inside.

Just before his face splintered Long Horn said, 'You do,' very quietly. And then the thing happened that always happened after that. The scene seemed to stop and scroll backwards. I saw an arrow going up and Long Horn laughing. I saw my bag drop on to the singing grass. After that I was back in the dazzle of light. Then I was back in the factory door.

The Glittering Star

I didn't say anything to Gran because she wouldn't believe me. She'd give me this look like she does sometimes, kind of soft and a bit wistful. She'd come out with one of her sayings, like 'You can't beat a bit of romancing, love.' It's what she says when she goes dancing with Ivy and has to pretend that she's a man.

Long Horn was mine alone, he'd told me so himself and he was a great sort of bloke to have on your side. Strong. Wild. Sure of himself. Except I'd still want Bach and Mozart and telescopes to look at the stars.

When I got home Gran's dancing shoes were in the hall. They're gold with high heels and straps up the front and they were standing there like Cinderella's slippers, only bigger and less sparkly than that. The Carpenters were singing *Your Love Has Put Me at the Top of the World*. She was quick-stepping round the room with her arms held up to an imaginary man.

Or maybe she saw my grandad. He had died before I was born and his photo's in a passe-partout frame on the mantelpiece.

'I'm feeling lucky today,' she said when she saw me. There was a smell of stew coming from the kitchen. 'I got a full house at bingo, Geoffrey, and I reckon Moira might share her bloke tonight. Doris won't. She's that mean she won't let him out of her sight for a minute. Come and give us a dance, love, will you? And then we'll go and have that stew.'

I don't mind dancing with Gran when we're on our own. As a matter of fact, I quite like it. For someone who's plump, she's light on her feet, so I took my blazer and jumper off and went up and put my arm round her waist. She took hold of my other hand in one of hers and we quick-stepped between the sofa and the china cabinet. Gran hummed a bit to some of the music and closed her eyes. 'You're a nifty dancer, our Geoffrey,' she said. Her waist felt soft and slippery under my hand. There was a flowery smell coming off her skin, but she'd still got the curler in her hair.

When the music finished she gave a great sigh. 'Go and wash your hands, Geoffrey. I'll get that stew from the oven now.'

Gran went out after supper with her dancing shoes in a plastic bag.

'Enjoy yourself,' I said to her.

She laughed and pinched my cheek and said, 'Mind what you get up to while I'm out.'

I did my homework and then went up to bed early. I hoped I would dream about Long Horn. He was in my head like a small, bright star you could almost touch if you wanted to, but that dream didn't come. Instead I dreamed of Mum and Dad. They were in Africa and they were helping somebody to build a boat. You could see the bare bones of it on the grass like an animal that's been picked dry by birds. Mum and Dad were laughing but I was suddenly afraid. I was afraid they'd get into that boat and sail away and never come back.

After that I didn't dream of anything.

The next morning I went off to school and in the afternoon we had double Art. Art's something I'd ordinarily like, but going into the Art room now's the same as going into hell. The kids mess about and act up all the time and Psycho Shane's been put in with us. Shane's terrifying. He's an un-human being. He's like a hurricane with a furious shout. 'Goggle-eyes!' he shouts at me straight away, and he comes up and tries to knock my specs off and Miss Carter tells him to go and sit down.

Only Shane never sits down and Miss Carter knows it and she says to him in a dead weary voice, 'For the second time, find a seat, Shane, please.' But instead of that he zooms round the room tipping things up and swearing at people until he winds himself up to such a pitch he can't even stay inside the room. You can hear him whooping down the corridor, slamming all the doors.

Michelle's the only one who can sort Shane out. She just says something and gives him a stare out of her scornful black-ringed eyes. But that day Michelle just picked at a nail and yawned while Miss Carter tried to calm him down.

As well as Shane there's Darren. Nobody ever looks at Darren because if he sees you looking he says, 'What do *you* want?' And you know what *he* wants is to beat you up. Darren looks like a bullet with a gold earring.

After Shane went off yelling Miss Carter said we were doing Utopia. 'Does anyone know what Utopia is?'

Darren climbed on a bench behind her back and ran along it rattling the blinds.

'Well, Utopia's a kind of paradise. It's the most perfect place you can imagine. What sort of places can you think of?'

The door opened then and the Head came in with Mr Humphrey who's big and red with a face like a fist. They walked up to Darren and bundled him out and Miss Carter said, 'Well?' in a shaky voice.

'A hip-hop concert, Miss, OK!'

'Nah! The Back Street Boys!' another kid said. A scuffle broke out between the two kids and Miss Carter said, ignoring them, 'Well, just think of a really beautiful place. Imagine you are there right now. Think about the shapes and the colours you'll find, and do your best to paint it for me.' Miss Carter's voice had that wistful note in it that Gran has when she talks about Grandad.

I sat at the back with Peter and Craig. They're quieter than most of the other kids. They're not friends of mine, because nobody at school is, but they don't give me hassle either.

Without speaking to them I fixed a bit of paper on my block and then thought about Utopia. Mum and Dad had said Africa was their Utopia and I tried to imagine hot sun and palm trees and parrots flying about. But the nightmare came back and I saw them sailing away in the skeleton boat, so I decided to think about Gran instead. Going to a dance with a bloke for once and whisking round the room with her eyes shut tight and her feet doing complicated dancey steps. That's Utopia for Gran.

I thought about the stars. When you look at the stars you're looking at the past. Not being here at all but being instead a brilliant light burning in a sea of dark. That's my Utopia; it has to be. I started to paint Alpha Centauri and make it into a dazzling horse. A star with burning silver wings instead of just the faint blur you can see when you look at it at the Observatory. But instead of me painting the star, the star seemed almost to be painting me.

This hugely glittering star appeared on the paper. Not Centaurus. It was more like the star I'd seen on the wall. The light from it seemed to reflect on my face and in the middle of it was a ring of fire.

I didn't paint that ring of fire, I swear it. Looking at it was like watching myself. Only not the self I was right now, but the self I always wanted to be.

And I knew without knowing how or why that Long Horn had painted that star for me.

A shadow fell over my desk and Miss Carter said, 'That's brilliant, Geoffrey, really,' in her weary, spaced-out sort of voice.

I nearly crumpled it up right then. Instead I shoved it in her hand and said, 'Here. You can keep it. I did it for you.'

After that it was time to go home. And I knew I had to find Long Horn again.

The factory seemed dead ordinary in the daylight and I felt daft being there, because what if I'd pretended Long Horn like I did pretend stuff sometimes? The pretending started when Mum and Dad went away and mostly it was stupid stuff, like I was playing the trumpet in a concert hall or going on a spacecraft up to Mars. You could pretend all you liked, that's what I thought, as long as no one ever found out. Only I'd never pretended a person before. Or not someone like Long Horn, anyway.

It was cold in the factory entrance. And dark. But the star glowed on the wall like a fire was lit inside it. The fire disappeared as soon as I looked, and so did the star. In their place there was a huge sun, blazing, and you could smell summer like a dry, sweet smell in your nose.

I was back on the plain and the grass was taller than it had been. It was so high it nearly reached my waist. There was a shushing noise where the wind went through it and overhead clouds were forming in the fierce blue sky and then slowly drifting away.

To begin with I couldn't see Long Horn. Then I heard his laugh. 'Over here, Magic Eyes! I need your help, my friend, today!'

Moving through the long green grass was like running through mud, you had to do it very slowly or you kept falling over and getting stuck. Long Horn was shouting, 'You were in my dreams last night, my friend. I knew that you would come today!' Then he gave another echoey laugh and said, 'Turn your toes in! Make your feet flat! Put your arms above your head!'

Feeling stupid, I put my bag up over my head and turned my toes in like a crab and slowly moved through the grass. I reached a river with clear water and Long Horn was on the bank on a horse with another boy. They were leading a second horse with a rope and they rode into the water. The green grass and blue sky were reflected in the spray. It was that hot I took my blazer off.

When they were in the water and the horses were chest

high, Long Horn suddenly shouted again, 'Quick, my friend – come over here! This one is going to fight, you'll see!'

He slipped off the leading horse and quickly climbed on to the second one. The other boy passed the rope to him and immediately the horse began to buck and kick. You could see Long Horn's muscles straining taut and his black hair flicking round his face.

'Come quick, my friend! You will help, I know!'

I nearly didn't dare to go. The sun made rainbows on my glasses and sweat was trickling down my arms and I'm scared of horses anyway.

But I took my shoes and socks off and rolled up my trouser legs. Then I pulled my jumper and shirt off so the sun felt hot on my bare white back and I went dashing in to the clear water, even though it was icy cold.

The horse was bucking and tossing its head. When I got to him Long Horn reached down a hand and I clambered up awkwardly, falling about and trying to keep my head out of the water, on to the horse's slippery back. And immediately it began to buck again. We were plunged back into the icy stream and my glasses got splashed so I couldn't see. I was holding on to Long Horn's waist and we slid down until we hit the horse's tail and Long Horn was laughing and yelling out loud, stuff like 'Haaa!' and 'Geeet!' and 'Yaaa!'

Then the horse plunged the other way and we slid on to its wiry mane. I could feel the tension in Long Horn's back, the way his ribs strained under the skin while the horse went on like a monster beast, puffing and blowing and rearing up. I could see the whites of its eyes and I nearly felt sorry for what we were doing, only suddenly *I* was yelling and screaming, 'Git on there! Yee-haa! Hup! Hup!'

Suddenly you could feel the hard knots on the horse's back relax and we were sitting in the quiet water with the quiet horse trembling under our thighs.

Long Horn pushed the hair back from his face. I could see a bone ring going through his ear, and the ring was like a red half-moon. The water was getting dry on our backs and the sun was making arrow shadows slanting out of the spiky grass.

'We work well together, Magic Eyes.' Long Horn turned round and laughed and then kicked the horse gently with his heels. We rode easily out of the water on to the grass. 'We give him a present now, yes? Magic Eyes? We let him take us like the wind.'

Without waiting for an answer Long Horn kicked the horse harder in the ribs. Long Horn's hair was in my face and the Plain was whirling yellow and green. We rode along the short grass by the river until we turned a corner and came to a camp. It was like some mega town with dogs and kids and tents everywhere. There were men smoking pipes and babies crawling. Women were working on skins stretched out and little kids played on hobby horses.

We circled the camp with Long Horn whooping and yelling 'Haaa!' while the horse's hooves pounded the turf and people turned to look at us. Then suddenly Long Horn pulled on the rope and the horse stopped abruptly and reared upon its back legs. I could feel myself slipping down and down and a man came out of one of the tents and stared at us with silent eyes.

The horse went back down on four feet again and settled in to a puffing calm. And the man said slowly, with great pride, 'You have done well, my son, today.' He reached out a hand to touch the horse and Long Horn put his hand on top. For a long moment they stared at each other, unsmiling, but you could see the powerful way they felt. We were off after that, back to the river. Back to my jumper and my shirt, my shoes and my winter socks waiting for me like dead men's clothes.

Very slowly I put them on. And when I did the sun went dimmer, like it knew I was Geoffrey Parker again. I turned round to Long Horn, still on his horse, and looked up against the sun at his face.

I meant to say something but the spray went suddenly up in my face and I was back in front of the star on the wall and it looked just ordinary and flat. I started walking home but I felt strange. Kind of empty and flat. Like an important part of me was missing and I needed Long Horn to get it back.

Psycho Shane

When I got in Gran was just coming through the back door with a tray in her hand. 'Mr O'Keef's very poorly,' she said, 'Perhaps you could nip round and see him, Geoffrey. He'd like that, you know. It'd be a special kindness to him.'

Mr O'Keef lives two doors away. He's old and his wife died years ago. Gran sent me round to see him before. He sat on the sofa and his hands shook. There were boxes of pills on the side table and the house smelt of frowsty, unwashed hair, medicine and old men's clothes. Going to see him made this scared question mark rear itself up at the back of my head.

I expect Gran saw the look on my face because she said, 'Sometimes you have to do what's right, Geoffrey, and not just what you want to do.'

Then she softened and said, 'We've got meat pie for supper today. I'll do you some chips with it if you like.'

And I got this sudden picture of Mum.

Mum didn't look much like Gran, her mum, but she often sounded like her. We had a neighbour, once, who used to complain about our cat. He said it killed his roses. He'd chase it through the hedge in his garden, cussing and throwing stuff and making death threats before it got run over on the main road.

But then the neighbour became suddenly old. He sat on a bench outside a shop and Mum stopped the car to give him a lift. She said, 'You have to do what's right, Geoffrey, or how else could the world go round?' and she gave me her fierce, Gran sort of look.

Now I said, 'I'll go round and see him later on.'

Gran put a hand to the small of her back and stood up from peering in the oven. 'I knew you would, chick. You're a very kind lad.'

After that I stopped thinking about Mum because it stirred up some stuff I'd rather forget.

Instead I said, 'You been busy today then, Gran?'

Gran sat down heavily on a kitchen chair and said, 'I'm always busy, you know that. You have to keep active, that's the thing.' She poured some tea from a big brown pot and I saw her give me a sideways look. 'There's this gala, Geoffrey. It's Saturday week if I remember right. I'm going with Ivy, but, you know . . . there's some times when Ivy just won't *do*.'

'No,' I said.

'Geoffrey! I haven't even asked you yet!'

'I'm not going to dance with you at the gala, Gran. I'd feel stupid, and anyway, Saturday's my Observatory night.'

'Well, our Geoffrey, I don't know! I'm not asking you to dance all night. Just one special dance for the spotlight prize. It's the Caribbean Foxtrot, a right tricky one, and Ivy's too short for the twirls. You could . . .'

'No,' I said again. And maybe I said it more loudly than I intended because Gran stopped rattling her teaspoon and picked up her glasses and put them on. She peered at me over the top of them.

'I won't press you, Geoffrey, if that's how you feel. But I thought you'd come with me this weekend. We'll only be there for an hour or two. It'd give you a chance to meet the girls and it's afternoon, so that's all right. If you don't want to, I'll understand. Only, Ivy *will* keep stepping on my corns whenever we have to do a reverse.'

Gran knew she'd won before she'd even finished speaking.

'I'll think about it,' is what I replied, and Gran smiled and looked pleased and patted my hand.

But would psycho Shane go and dance with his gran? And what would Long Horn think if he knew?

Suddenly Gran made me jump. She said, 'You get your trousers wet today?'

I glanced down at them. They were wrinkled round the bottom and looked limp and damp.

'Can't remember,' I said, and shrugged. And Gran gave me another look like she knew I was lying, but all she said, was, 'You should learn to take more care of your clothes,'

Later on I went upstairs and played some Wagner really loud. While it was playing I wrote a letter:

> *Dear Mum and Dad,*
>
> *I hope you're OK. Why don't you write to me?*
>
> *Is it too far to send a letter? What's it like where you are now?*
>
> *When are you going to come for me?*
>
> *Hope you're OK and not missing me.*
>
> *Love from*
>
> *Geoffrey XX*

When I'd written the letter I read it through, and then drew a straight line under my name and put it on top of the other letters under my stamp album in the bottom drawer.

After that I switched off the music and got into bed. When I closed my eyes the indian on the pavement blazed in my head and stayed there until I heard Gran bolt the front door and start to climb heavily up the stairs.

We had Maths at school first thing in the morning and Maths is nearly as bad as Art, mainly because the teacher's scared. We were outside the room and kids were pushing and shoving and kicking each other, you could smell mucky feet and bubble gum and some stuff they use to clean the floors.

I was trying my best not to catch Darren's eyes while he did his bullet thing with some kids, butting into them with his head and yelling stuff like 'Weirdo!' and 'Creep!' But then the door opened and we all surged in and instead of it being like it usually is, just a scruffy space with metal desks and notices up saying,

> *Follow Maths instruction*
> *No fighting*
> *No playing*
> *No swearing*
> *No teasing*
> *No name-calling*
> *Leave others in peace*
> *Bring correct equipment*

There was this music floating into the room. It was nothing special, just Mozart's *Eine Kleine Nachtmusik* but hearing it then was like listening to a cool, clear river running gently past your ears while you were stuck inside some deep, thick mud.

I sat down at my desk while the music carried on playing. Some of the kids were pulling faces and looking at each other and then at Miss Sinclair, who stood at the front with an anxious smile. But the class settled down dead fast after that.

The aggro level nearly drained away and even Darren stopped pinching the back of another kid's neck and sat still with his arms folded on his chest and this angry, bewildered look on his face.

In a minute or two the music stopped and Miss Sinclair said, 'Well done, class eight, I haven't had to raise my voice once this morning. It's good to see you can behave.'

Immediately after she spoke there was this steady grumbling noise from the back and Michelle Morgan shouted out, 'What were you playing that to us for?'

She waited for Miss Sinclair to say something smart, but she didn't and Michelle shrugged and scowled and said, 'Well, why should I care if *you* don't know?'

Another wit said, 'That's rubbish, that is,' and looked round, grinning at the other kids.

Which is when Miss Sinclair made another mistake, she said, 'Call me Miss when you speak to me.'

And Michelle said, 'Fine. OK. Yes, Sir. Right,' which made everybody start laughing out loud and saying, 'Yes, Sir, OK. Fine,' while Miss Sinclair's voice began to wobble a bit and you could see she was trying her best to keep calm. She shouted out to us over the racket and banged her ruler down on the desk, 'Can anyone tell me what the music was?'

And instead of keeping quiet, like I should have done, I put my hand up and shouted back, 'Yes, Miss. It was Mozart. It was the *Eine Kleine Nachtmusik*.'

Miss Sinclair looked at me as if I'd done a magic trick. Just when I wanted her to let it go she said eagerly, 'Brilliant. Thank you, Geoffrey, dear! Are you into classical music or was it simply a lucky guess?'

Behind me Darren was just revving up, saying, 'Brilliant, Geoffrey! You're a star!' in a stupid, high-pitched voice.

Miss Sinclair was still waiting for me to answer with this hopeful, don't-let-me-down sort of smile. But I'm the one who has to live with class eight. So I shrugged and said, scowling, 'No I'm not. It's some rubbish I heard on the radio.'

From under my eyebrows I watched Miss Sinclair deflate very gently. 'If that's the case, Geoffrey, you did well to remember.'

Which is when I got this sudden, clear picture of Long Horn laughing and calling me his friend. After that I felt something collapsing inside *me*. The idea that I could be Long Horn's friend seemed stupid and pathetic. I wasn't even as brave as Michelle Morgan with her scornful eyes and sod-you smile. And wherever I went nothing would change. I would still be me, Geoffrey Parker, nobody special and a coward.

I kept my head down for the next half hour. I was doing some geometry when Mr Bates came in and said, 'How did it go?' And Miss Sinclair replied, 'So much for Mozart. It didn't work. They're just as awful as they always are.'

For the rest of the day I got this stick, 'He-*llo*, Geoffrey.

How's teacher's pet?' 'Oh, Geoffrey, dear, you're *so* brilliant.' Michelle Morgan was the worst. She kept saying, 'I'm a kinda prat I am,' and I kept my face dead stiff and straight so in a while she got bored with it. But it made me remember the homework, that thing about the stupid prunes. And I didn't want to be noticed again.

At home time I wished I was in Africa, or going in a shuttle up to the moon. Or anywhere except Nottingham and Dame Watson Comprehensive School. So I went down to Hockley and stared at the star, but nothing happened.

I knew then that the indian had found me out and decided to take Long Horn away for good.

Dancing with Gran

I was fed up again the next day. I kept remembering Mum and Dad and it was like pressing on a big raw patch and deliberately trying to make it worse.

I mooched downstairs and sat at the table. 'What's got eight letters and means withdraw?' Gran asked without looking up.

'Dunno,' I shrugged and crumbled some toast and Gran said impatiently, 'Well *think*, Geoffrey. If I don't get that I won't get four down: was bound to be, dash, caught.'

'Had,' I said, without thinking.

'There you are, I knew you could do it. You just have to apply yourself, that's the thing. We got one wrong yesterday, by the way, we put rub instead of dab and that gave us row instead of din. Now, what's the matter with you today, Geoffrey?'

Gran looked at me over the top of her specs and let a

small silence fall. When I didn't answer she reached a hand out across the table and put it gently over mine. Her hand felt warm and comfortable.

'Is it your mum and dad again? Or did something happen at school yesterday?'

For a moment I nearly told her about Miss Sinclair. Was I right or was I a coward? And what *about* my mum and dad? If I'd been OK would they have left? Or did they leave when they found me out, the same way as the indian did?

'Nothing happened,' I said sullenly.

Then her hand gave mine a soft, warm, squeeze. 'All right, Geoffrey,' was what she said. But there was a note of disbelief in her voice.

After that we went shopping and I carried Gran's heavy bags for her. I saw Michelle Morgan on the way home. She nudged at her friend and they laughed out loud and both turned round to look at me. I went bright red and they turned away, then Michelle looked back again over her shoulder and she wasn't laughing any more.

In the afternoon we went to the dance at the Community Centre. I had my jeans on and Gran looked but deliberately said nothing. She was wearing a pleated skirt in some shiny stuff and a lacy top she'd knitted herself. When we were nearly there Gran took my arm and pressed it against her best green coat. 'You're as tall as me now, Geoffrey,' she said. 'I'm right glad that you've come with me.'

Inside the hall there were lots of ladies, some of them with gentlemen.

'Is that your young man?' they said to Gran, and Gran was smiling and nodding and looking proud. Then the ladies sat down and took their proper shoes off and strapped themselves into dancing shoes.

I looked out of the window and my heart gave a bang because some girls were on our school playing-field. They were trying to get a ball in a net and jostling each other while they jumped up and down. But I twigged pretty soon they weren't in my year so it's likely they wouldn't know who I was.

After that I tried to relax and read a notice on the wall: 'Do Not Attach Any Other Notice to This Board.' There was a picture underneath it with people on and how to resuscitate them.

Next the teacher came swooping in, all beaming and shiny and out of breath. 'Hello, one and all!' she shouted out. Then she spotted Gran and me, 'We'll have to have a Ladies' Excuse Me today!'

Somebody yelled, 'How-do there, Beryl! We'll excuse you, duck, any time!' Then Beryl went diving round the room, laughing and joking and saying stuff like, 'Are you going to take your cardy off, John?' and somebody wolf-whistled when he did. Then Beryl said, 'Have you all got off what you're taking off?' and the same joker la-laa-ed *The*

Stripper dead loud, and Beryl said, 'Harold's taking his tie off, folks!'

After that she put some music on and all at once it was like a rush of magic. The people who were nattering on went quiet suddenly and sat straight and still in their chairs. Their eyes went dreamy. It was as if they'd run away to when they were young and maybe it was better this time round.

Next thing, Beryl's on the floor, dancing with Derek. 'This is the Monet Waltz,' she called. She floated round in her high-heeled shoes and when she'd been round twice, the others joined in.

Gran was with Ivy being the man. Everyone was doing the same fancy steps at exactly the same beat in the music, at exactly the same split second of time. It was almost as good as being with Long Horn.

I gave a sigh and Beryl winked, then the music finished and Gran came up. She said, 'Perhaps you could do a swing-time later? Only if you want to, like.'

Up until then my legs had been crossed and my arms folded firmly over my chest, and I reckon I'd had a scowl on my face. But suddenly I said, 'Sure. OK. If you like.'

The next dance was the Mayfair Quickstep, and then a saunter and Beryl shouted out, 'Saunter together, ladies and gents, saunter together, if you please.'

She was dancing with a lady and they were doing all the turns and flourishes and humming along to the soft, slow tune. When it finished Beryl took the lady back to her seat and said very loudly, 'Where's Vera today? Not taken poorly again, I hope'

'She's got roots in her drains,' a bald man said. 'She'll likely be back next week, Beryl, love.'

We had tea after that, with bourbon biscuits and custard creams, and Beryl fanned her face and chatted to me. 'We tend to lose the gentlemen first, but it's grand the ladies still come here. They make friends you see. It gets them out. They enjoy themselves and that's great, that is. It makes it all worth while for me.' She took a bite from a custard cream and leaned a bit closer in and said, 'Your gran's really proud of you, Geoffrey.'

I looked out of the window again. The light was fading and dark was coming in swirly grey drifts. The girls were just finishing off their game and they bobbed up and down like ghostly grey ships. And I reckon I wanted to say something then, but was worried in case my voice sounded weird. What I wanted to say was, 'D'you think I could come and live with you?'

Stupid. Pathetic. Not what I meant.

But Beryl looked as if she would never have to be on her own unless she really wanted to.

I said nothing and Beryl got up to go. She said, 'Righty-oh then, ladies and gents. No rest for the wicked. Time for you to go back to work!'

Beryl laughed as the music started up and clapped her hands and said, 'Leave all your troubles behind you now!'

'I've brought mine with me!' a lady said. She pointed at her husband and everyone laughed, and a lady in a tiger-patterned blouse said, 'I'll take him off your hands, if you like!'

I was dancing with Gran. It was the Sycamore Swing and we stamped and clapped and shouted 'Hoy!' while Gran beamed and nodded and went very flushed and sang along to *Have a Drink on Me*. Then I danced with Ivy who was looking sad and said, 'You remind me sometimes of my Stan.'

I left a bit early when the Tango came on and told Gran I was off to the Observatory. Beryl was saying, 'Step-forward. Whisk. Slow. Man-turn.' She gave me a wave when I went out the door and some of the ladies blew me a kiss.

And I knew I meant to go and find Long Horn again. But when I got down Hockley the star didn't change. I stared at it and waited a while. I saw it flicker once and switch itself off. Then I turned round and went off to the Observatory.

Brian was watching a film in the TV room.

'Hey-up, lad – you're just in time to see a star being made.' He shuffled up to make room for me as a star exploded on to the screen.

I sat down without taking my eyes off the star, and in a second forgot about everything else.

* * *

Next morning I woke up early. Gran was lying in bed singing *Onward Christian Soldiers* like she usually did on a Sunday and the noise was floating in through the wall. Once when she sang it the Salvation Army struck up in the street outside. Gran thought it was some kind of miracle and leaned out of the window in her curlers and sang along even louder.

Now it was quiet outside. I got out of bed and went downstairs. If Mum and Dad had still been here we'd have gone for a drive in the country. We'd have had a picnic and Dad would have said, 'That's a burial mound, look, over there,' and Mum would have gone all moony and said, 'Fancy, Geoffrey, all those people gone before us. It makes you think a bit, doesn't it?'

But they weren't here and I thought about writing them another letter and decided they didn't deserve one yet, so I made some tea and took some to Gran in her favourite cup with the roses on.

'You've saved my life, Geoffrey,' she said. Gran sat up slowly in her flowered nightie and looked at me over the rim of the cup and said, 'I've a use for you today, my duck.'

Without her teeth Gran looked even older than usual, like her ice-creamy face had just melted away, and I got this sudden twist of something. Not fear, but more like a guilty kind of wishing when I thought about Beryl so glowing and strong in the middle of a smiling family.

'Oh yeah?' I said. And my voice seemed to echo in Gran's room like a lonely chord on an out-of-tune piano.

'This afternoon, if you don't mind, love. We should have a go at the Caribbean Foxtrot. Just make a start, like, to see how things go.'

'OK,' I said, and turned away and went downstairs and drank some tea and wondered why things had to change. I like stuff to always stay the same because you know where you are when that happens. You may not be happy, or not all the time, but you feel you're where you really belong and nothing can bother you all that much.

I went upstairs and got my prune juice homework out. A couple of old folks looking glum in cardigans with a banner over the top saying, 'LACKING ENERGY? FEELING OLD? Cast off that over-fifty feeling! Grow old disglacefully. Drink PRUNE JUICE!' Then a picture of the same couple with flowers in their teeth tangoing together in a room full of happy smiling people. 'Feeling Healthy! Feeling Good! Having the energy to get up and go! That's what HARVEST PRUNE JUICE does for you! 100% natural. No added sugar. Drink HARVEST PRUNE JUICE and get a life of your own!'

It was like having acne and being given the advert for Clearasil. Psycho Shane would duff me up in the showers.

For a while I just sat and looked at it and hated Miss Turner and all of class eight. But then out of the blue I got this flash like a sudden, brilliant shock to my brain.

Something I'd never had before except when I saw the Blazing Star.

You don't have to do it if you don't want to!

I decided I would do another ad, say for Macdonald's or Burger King. Miss Turner wouldn't remember, or if she did I'd just bluff it out and act up like the other kids did.

But then I was fed up some more. It's like bits of Long Horn had rubbed off on me, but not enough to make any real difference, only enough to scare me and make me feel strange inside my skin. I nearly scrabbled in the waste-paper basket to try and stick the advert together again. To stop myself doing it I went down Hockley Lane.

The factory was closed. Across the entry there was an iron gate. I could see the star through it but I couldn't get in, so I rattled the gate and then went back home.

Gran was doing the dinner. 'Set that table, Geoffrey,' she said. 'And don't look so miserable, you've got your health.'

We ate our dinner while Gran talked. 'I'd go to church,' she said, chewing, 'only that new vicar's a real fly-boy. There was a guitar last week and we had to clap. It's not Christian, clapping like that in church.'

After dinner I did the washing-up while Gran went to have a lie down on her bed. She got up in time for *Sing Something Simple* and played along to it on a paper and comb. For a while you could hear stuff coming out like *Beautiful Dreamer* and *I Only Have Eyes For You*, then she sighed and put the soggy paper down. 'I can't get the tone right now, Geoffrey. It's these new teeth. They're not fixed right. Never mind. It's an ill wind blows. We'll have a go at that foxtrot instead. Come on, Geoffrey, there's a good lad.'

In the living room we pushed the sofa back and Gran said, 'Right. We'll have a go without the music, just to see how we get on.'

She was still wearing an apron that said Chief Pot Washer in letters made up of dishes and knives. I could feel the knot of it at the back of her waist where I clutched at it with my right hand. My left hand was held very firmly in Gran's.

'The way it goes,' she said, 'is slow, slow, quick-quick, slow quick-quick, step, hover and turn. Feather finish and three step. Right, Geoffrey, I'll hum three times and then you step.'

Gran hummed and I stepped slowly forward and then quick-quicked and stepped again. When it came to the hover Gran said sharply, '*Hover*, Geoffrey, don't stop dead. You're dancing, remember, not driving something. Now do it again from the last step.'

We did it again and I got the turn wrong. 'You'll knock me for six if you keep doing that. Now come on, our Geoffrey, concentrate.'

'I'd do it better if you were wearing shoes,' I said, and Gran snorted and gave me a withering look. 'You'd do it better if you listened,' she said.

At the end of another half-hour she let go of my hand. 'You'll do, Geoffrey. For now. Tomorrow we'll go through it all again. Nose to the grindstone. Back to the wheel. When you've got it right we'll do the next steps. Ooh, our Geoffrey, just you wait – what a pair we'll make on Gala Night!'

I went upstairs early after tea, mostly because I was tired and bored and because the day had seemed to be mostly full stops. If Dad was here I'd have told him about it because Dad was someone you could tell things to. He explained things to me, patiently. He explained about what made black holes, about the core of things collapsing and dying and about gravity becoming so strong that nothing could escape from it, not even abstract stuff like light.

I put some music on, *Chaos* from Haydn's *The Creation*, and got into bed. I let the music pound in the room while I looked at Jupiter outside the window and wished again I was somewhere else, with Mum and Dad in Africa sitting under the Southern Cross.

Remembering Dad

We had Maths again on Monday and the regular teacher was off. In her place was another one, small and thin with short dark hair.

'Who are you?' Michelle Morgan asked.

'Who I am and why I am here is none of your business,' the teacher said. 'Now, get your work books out, and carry on quietly where you left off.'

'Listen to her!' someone shouted out and the teacher fixed them with a long, cold stare.

I was going to do some algebra, but couldn't be bothered to concentrate so I read the notices on the wall instead. One of them said 'MISS SINCLAIR'S SUPER-DOUPER STAMPS' on top of a stupid sort of chart you do for little kids, with pictures and some words explaining. There were two cats for *Purrfect. Full marks. 2 merits*. A bumble bee with *Bee neat. Please improve*. And a thumbs-up meaning *Very good. 3 merits*.

The teacher was flicking through a magazine confiscated from one of the girls. I saw her flick on to a page that had a picture of a long-haired girl and a headline saying 'It's Your First Date. How Far Should You Go?' In between flicking she was looking up and shouting stuff out like, 'Stay in your seats! Put up your hand if you want to speak!'

When I'd read the chart I read another notice saying, 'Severe Clause. Any pupil whose behaviour is threatening or puts themselves or others at risk will be removed from the room.'

After that I did some work but my chair kept getting kicked from behind and Darren was scowling and hissing at me, 'Who's a smart-arse music prat?'

Later when we were waiting for an English lesson to start I saw Sharon Daly giggle with her mates. Then one of them came up and flicked at my specs and said, 'I'm a stupid music prat.' And that made everyone else start up, singing out loud in a daft sort of voice, 'I'm a stupid music prat, la la la.'

In English a note went round the room saying 'Geoffrey's gran made him a prat. If I get her the wool, will she make me one too?'

At four o'clock I went round to the factory and stared at the star.

And I went off straight away. I didn't even have to concentrate before I was there.

I was on a hill with snow knee-deep and Long Horn in front of me, standing still.

He saw me immediately.

'Magic Eyes! I wished for you and you came to me!' And perhaps it was because he was wearing more clothes, leggings and a kind of cape, that he seemed bigger again.

'Well,' I said, feeling awkward. My skin was starting to shrink with the cold and the air felt thin and shrill with it.

Long Horn laughed and crunched towards me through the snow. His cape was decorated with moons and stars and he put his arm round my shoulders the way you wouldn't dare with your mates at school.

'Come and see what I have made for you! Only now have I finished it. And I wait, Magic Eyes, for you to share this with me.'

His arm round my shoulders was like a strange kind of force, propelling me with him through the snow. We went up the hill with fir trees on it weighted down with piles of snow, and at the top he suddenly made a gesture and a heap of snow fell away from something.

It was a kind of sledge made out of the rib-cage of a large animal, a buffalo, maybe, and over the bones was a dark brown hide. There was a raw-hide rope at the front of it and a tail sticking crazily out behind.

'See! You and me will have fun today! But first there is something I have to do.'

Long Horn grabbed the rope and pulled the sledge round and round in snow cloud circles, laughing and shouting so his breath plumed out and made wild smoke rings in the air. Then he jumped on a seat made out of skin and leaned well back with his legs forward.

'Now you come, Magic Eyes!' he yelled.

I took my glasses off and huffed on them to melt the ice-patterns starting to form, and to gain some time because I was scared again. Besides that, I was so cold I almost couldn't breathe for the ice that was settling in my lungs. Only, I couldn't not go, or Long Horn might dump me for good this time.

I got on the sledge and we started off, whizzing along in the blinding snow with tree poles looming up in front and the sledge bones making an icy whoosh. Long Horn was laughing and whooping out loud and suddenly my scared feeling disappeared like something that had got left behind. I even stopped feeling cold and lay back with my feet braced up and the rope in my hand making the sledge go faster and faster so you thought you were flying. And the sun came out in a sudden flash and lit the snow up like mountain fire so the trees and the peaks seemed to blaze crimson flames.

When we could see again we were in a valley. It was suddenly quiet and even Long Horn grew stiller and taller. By then the sun had dropped again and the trees were looming like dark grey ghosts and I nearly didn't see Long Horn's father, standing on the track in front of us. In the background there were other kids playing, pulling skins along the ground and taking it in turns to sit, but you couldn't hear them and his father seemed to hold his own kind of quiet that would go with him wherever he went.

We stopped in front of him and he didn't move. He just looked at us with long, still eyes. 'My father,' said Long Horn, with unsmiling reverence. Around us there was the creak of trees shifting and the snow started falling in soft, feathery flakes. Very slowly his father inclined his head and you felt something, like power coming into you. Then Long Horn bent his own head in a kind of bow. After that the snow fell faster and faster. It whirled around us in an icy storm and I was rushing down the slopes again, I was crunching over towards Long Horn, I was feeling afraid and very cold.

I stood in front of the star again and my clothes were sticking to me with the damp. I wondered what I would say to Gran, but as luck would it have she wasn't in. She was taking Mr O'Keef's dinner again and I got changed into some other clothes and put my school stuff on the radiator.

When Gran came in she was looking sad. 'That daughter of his, she never comes.' Gran shook her head and pursed her lips. 'It's no use saying she lives away. There's duty, Geoffrey. That's what folks forget.'

She put some potatoes on the stove and said, 'I could do

with five minutes now, Geoffrey, just to start feeling right again. We'll have a go at that foxtrot, shall we? Just while the spuds are starting to do.'

She put *Hello Mary Lou* on and we did the first few steps to it, and Gran said, 'Make sure you do three steps in a line. And remember, Geoffrey, this is a person you're leading, you know, not a blooming great cart-horse.'

Later I went off to do my homework. I put part three of *The Creation* on and thought about the advert again. I might not do Macdonald's, just in case all those Big Macs could get picked on by Michelle and turned against me into one of her jokes. Michelle jokes a lot, but she only laughs sometimes as if she means it, and when she does it makes her look different. I heard someone say that her folks have split and she's mostly always on her own. So maybe there's not much to laugh about. But I saw her laughing when the music started, one of *The Creation*'s best bits where Adam sings,

'Brightest of stars, how beautifully dost thou herald the day.'

Gran was ill the next day, although she was up when I went downstairs. She was coughing a bit and there was a wheeze at the end of the cough that made my stomach clench.

'Geoffrey,' she said, 'there's some porridge for you.'

'You should be in bed,' I told her. 'I could stay off school and look after you.'

'You'll do no such thing.' Gran tutted indignantly and lifted up the edge of the tea cosy. She felt the brown pot with the palm of her hand and her wedding ring looked looser than it usually did. Usually it's buried in her finger with pink soap stuck round the rim of it, but now when I saw it I started to get worried again. Can a person get thinner overnight? If they could, then other things might happen. Gran might get iller and iller and I might not be there to notice it. She might . . .

'Geoffrey!' Gran said sharply. 'Eat your porridge and stop looking dim. You're late today and I won't have you go missing school. This here tea's still hot in the pot, so get it down you and hurry up!'

Gran went round the kitchen doing things, and I ate my porridge feeling guilty because I reckoned Gran wasn't where she wanted to be. I reckoned Gran wanted a bungalow. One of those new ones set in a square up Colwick Road. They have cords to pull in all the rooms so you can call someone to help you out. They've central heating and an electric fire like a real one flickering with plastic coals.

'There's these things on the bath to give you a lift if you're stiff and need some extra pull. And they're warm, Geoffrey. They've got double-glazing so you can't hear the noise going on outside. There's a garden to sit in and they've got high toilet seats. Ivy's got her name down for one.'

Gran told me this a few weeks ago after she'd been to

look at them. Since then I felt like I was holding her back, because if it weren't for me, Gran could have put *her* name down. She could have a warden and an over-bath pulley and go off to Eastbourne with her dancing group.

I gave a sigh and Gran said, 'Look sharp! And come straight home today, Geoffrey. There might be an errand or two for you. Now, have you got all your gear ready to go? Well, hoppit then, go on – you'd better run!'

School was just as bad as ever. Psycho Shane was with us again and we had Food Technology which meant making a salad.

'You put the green leaves in the bottom of the bowl, then the rest of the salad ingredients on top so you've colour and form and it looks good to eat. After that you can . . .'

Mr Jones didn't get any further because a tomato went whizzing past his ear and guess who threw it? It would have to be Michelle, who gave one of her laughs, and then threw it to Shane so he was encouraged to throw some more. Soon there's stuff whizzing everywhere and Mr Jones stops trying to teach the lesson and says, 'That's enough, everyone, settle down. Shane's not being clever today at all.'

The trouble is, you don't *learn* anything, and no one seems to care if you don't, so I sat where I was and worried about Gran, and carried on worrying until it was time to go home.

When I got in it was very quiet. There was a plate on the

table in the living room with half a sardine sandwich on it and a digestive biscuit, broken in two.

'Gran?' I said.

'I'm up here, love.'

Gran was lying on the bed with the green quilt pulled up over her. And I guess something must have shown in my face because she said, nettled, 'I'm only having a rest, Geoffrey. I didn't realise it was that time already. Now, will you go to Boots and get some linctus – it's the yellow one, the girl will know. And don't let them fob you off with their own stuff. It tastes like creosote and you can't get it down.'

I went straight out. It was October and nippy with the nights drawing in. You could see the Plough again, and if you looked carefully you could see Mizar, the second star from the left with another, fainter one called Alcor. A double star. I stopped where I was to look at them. You could only see Mizar through a telescope, but looking at them made me think of Dad.

When I'd looked enough I went to Boots and got Gran's linctus and the lady there said, 'She wants to take care. There's a lot of this flu going around now.'

At home Gran was in the kitchen again. She said, 'It's just salad and jacket potatoes tonight. You'll have to take Mr O'Keef's dinner to him, I daren't risk him getting any bugs of mine.'

She put a tray into my hands with dishes on covered with

a checked tea towel. 'Make sure and give him my love, Geoffrey – tell him I'll likely be round tomorrow when my medicine's had time to do its job.'

I went down the alley and round the back to Mr O'Keef's kitchen door. 'It's only me! Gran sent me round because she's not too well.'

I went in the dark kitchen and you could smell gas and old dinners, and some long drawers were hanging on a line near the sink.

'Come in, lad.'

Mr O'Keef was sitting where I remembered him from last time, almost as if he'd never moved. He was even wearing the same clothes, old tweed trousers with a jacket and shirt, and a scarf tucked into the top of his shirt. His hands were shaking when he took the tray and you could see brown marks on the back of them.

'She's a grand lass, your gran,' he said into his scarf. 'You want to take care of her, you do.'

The table next to him was still covered with bottles and I whipped the tea towel off the tray and backed away as fast as I could.

'Gran says she'll be back tomorrow, maybe.'

'Aye. Well. If she ain't I shall manage, young man. Tell her.'

He picked his knife and fork up and I went back into the dark kitchen and let myself out again.

Gran and me went to bed early that night. We didn't even practise the Caribbean Foxtrot and that was worse than having Gran shout at me.

To stop myself worrying about her I thought of Long Horn. I wondered what he saw in me, because he was all the things I wanted to be but never could. Then I remembered Dad again. We'd been looking at Mizar and Dad said, 'Always remember *you're* brilliant, Geoffrey. You're a double star to me and your mum.'

The Killing

A weird thing happened at school the next day. I must have been humming something because Darren came up in the corridor and tried to head-butt me. At the same time as his head came out he said, 'You're a dick-head music prat.' Only before he'd managed to do all that my hand went up and clocked him one. He fell back against the wall and he wasn't hurt, only surprised, but Mr Peters had spotted me. I had to stay out in the corridor during the lesson.

Being outside wasn't that bad. Better than being *inside*. It was quieter, nobody gave you any hassle. Soon there were four of us standing outside. We played poker for chewing gum and crisps and I won because I look like a prat.

Darren said later, 'I'm going to get you, prat.' And I thought, well, go on, then. Do it. Then I'll get you back and be caught again and stay outside and enjoy myself. But he mooched away and I ate the crisps I'd won and thought he'd likely forget about me because Darren doesn't remember much.

After school I went straight home to Gran. She was still coughing but not as much, and we managed a few of the foxtrot steps in between going round to Mr O'Keef's and sitting down to eat our dinner.

Gran said, 'Your reverses are getting better, Geoffrey. But your feathering's just a mite off course.'

Then after dinner the phone rang. It was Brian from the Observatory. He said, 'You OK Geoffrey? Only I saw you weren't there Saturday.'

And I said, 'I'm OK. Gran's not too well.'

'You can see Pleiades right clear tonight. I thought we might go. Can we pick you up?'

I was going to say no when Gran chipped in. 'Who's that ringing? Brian, is it? Tell him you're going if he's asking you out. It might stop you moping and do you some good.'

At seven o'clock Brian honked outside and I got in the car all muffled up in two layers of woollies and a stripy hat Gran knitted for me last birthday. In the car Brian said, 'How-do,' Kenneth nodded and Maureen grinned. We set off through the fag-end of town, then out through some woods and up to the hill with the Observatory dome on top of it.

When I see that dome my stomach lurches, only not with nerves. More like when you know something brilliant's going to happen and you're waiting for it. We got out the car and you could see lights in the distance in Nottingham, twinkling yellow and white with the city blur round them. Without speaking we went to the dome and unlocked the door.

'Coffee?' said Brian.

I nodded at him and he went into the little kitchen and brought back four steaming mugs of it. After that he put some music on and I was pleased because the others were wearing anoraks and woolly hats like me. The music he put on was a Bach cello suite and Maureen and Kenneth nodded again and smiled and said, 'That's right good, that is. We like that, Brian.'

Brian was wearing a green jumper tucked into his trousers and there was dinner down the front of it. The ends of his sleeves were frayed, but Brian smiled and nodded his head to the music and his quiet was like talking would be with other people.

We went up to the dome, which looks just like a big white super-golf ball. Brian pressed a switch and the roof cranked back and it was like that rush of magic again. All you could see was the huge sky and stars. You couldn't hear anything except for Bach.

'It's the harbinger of winter, that is,' said Kenneth. He was looking at the sky through binoculars. 'They're all there tonight, all seven of them.'

He passed the binoculars over to me and I looked to the east and saw Pleiades like an open jewel box. As I said before:

when you look at the stars you're looking at the past and maybe that's why I think it's so great, you might get back all the best bits you want to remember.

I tried *not* to remember when Mum and Dad left. I was stood on my own in the living room and the house seemed full of things I didn't recognise; chairs I couldn't remember sitting on and pictures I hadn't seen before. Even the walls and the doors looked like they were someone else's. It's only when I look at the stars I can remember the good stuff properly again.

I looked at Pleiades as if I was looking at our room. Mum was doing a jigsaw puzzle because it helped her to think and Dad was arranging bits of bone and muttering to himself. Nothing happened. It was summer and the light was starting to fade and it was OK doing nothing in particular.

'All right, Geoffrey?'

Brian moved the great telescope up a bit. 'I've got her. She's brilliant. Take a look.'

Maureen peered through the telescope and let out a gasp. 'I don't recall seeing her like that before.'

She looked a bit longer and then climbed down and Kenneth went up to the little platform. 'She's a beauty,' he said. 'The seventh sister. You can usually see only six of those stars. Fantastic! Geoffrey. Come and look. You'll never see Pleiades like this again.'

The seventh sister was there, a blazing dazzle of silver.

There was a blue glow round her like a nimbus, and even though I know it's just dust reflected in the starlight it made tears come into my eyes.

Downstairs Bach was still playing. I was looking at the seventh star when the blue round it began to change to purple and red and then blazed deep crimson with spits of fire. Goose bumps came up on my skin.

Right after that the indian appeared. Not Long Horn with his clear white laugh, but the indian on the pavement. Huge. Terrifying. With blazing eyes and red stripes on his face. He was in the sky looking down at me and for one split second we stared at each other.

Behind me I heard Brian say something but his voice was just a sound against my ear. When he spoke the indian began to fade. The red went to purple and back to blue and the seventh sister was there again.

'Good, eh?' said Brian.

I came down from the platform and the others were standing there smiling comfortably with mugs in their hands.

I saw the indian again when I was lying in bed, but only in my imagination.

Then I remembered Long Horn that first time. I remembered me saying to him, 'I don't know you.'

And Long Horn saying quietly, '*You do.*'

* * *

In the morning I wrote to Mum and Dad.

> *Dear Mum and Dad,*
> *What's it like where you are now? I expect it's hot,*
> *but it's very cold here. Perhaps I could come and see*
> *you soon? I've got a record you might like. I'll play*
> *it to you if you come.*
> *Love from*
> *Geoffrey XXX*

I left the letter on my desk and Gran came in later and saw it there. She said, 'Oh, Geoffrey,' and looked upset.

'I'm not going to post it,' I said, huffily. 'Don't get your knickers in a twist.'

'Knickers indeed! Well, I don't know! What a thing to say. I'd be ashamed if I were you, Geoffrey.'

Saying that made Gran forget to be upset and I put the letter on top of the others and slammed the door shut on to it.

At school Darren shoved my chair and I shoved it back, right into his stupid desk.

'Ow! That hurt! Miss!' he yelled.

'What's the matter?' Miss Turner said.

'He shoved my desk back on purpose, Miss.'

'Did you, Geoffrey?' Miss Turner asked.

'Might have done,' I said, darkly. 'And if he shoves my chair, I might do it again.'

'Ooh, Geoffrey,' some kids yelled.

Michelle shot me a look and almost smiled, then remembered who she was smiling at, and in a second I saw it fade.

Miss Turner looked like I'd stirred up her calm, but all she said was, 'Try to behave.' Then she went back to talking about adverbs.

At four o'clock I went straight home and Gran was just back from Mr O'Keef's.

'I've took him round some shepherd's pie.' Gran pursed her lips and shook her head. 'He's not as good as he was, you know. And care workers don't begin to make up, not for your own family.'

After that we had tea and Gran nattered on. 'There'll be a right good buffet on Gala Night. Scrimshaw's are going to do it for us, so you know everything will be really nice. There'll be candles on the tables, Geoffrey, and speeches and prizes for each dance. There'll be a real live band wearing decent clothes and balloons will come down at the end.'

Then after tea she said, 'Blow the pots! Let's have a go at that dance, Geoffrey.'

She put a tape on and got out her shoes with the gold straps and sparkly bits. And immediately she seemed different, somehow. Not just taller, but you could imagine Grandad calling her 'Sweetheart mine' like she says he did.

We danced to *Hello Mary Lou* again and Gran said, 'Right.

Gent steps back on right foot diagonal to centre . . . slow, quick-quick. Come on, Geoffrey, put some pep into it, lad.'

But after ten minutes she ran out of puff. You could hear her chest begin to wheeze and she said, 'I'd better have some of my medicine. And take that look off your face, Geoffrey. It's a cough I've got, not a death rattle.'

I washed the pots while Gran had a sit. But when I came in the living room I couldn't sit down. I fiddled around with the gas fire and flicked through a dog-eared *People's Friend*, but all the time I was aware of something happening I couldn't see. There was this snap of excitement; I kept needing to pee and my fingers were playing tunes on my leg.

In the end I couldn't stay in the house so I took myself off to the factory, but I just got as far as Hockley Lane. I was thinking about Long Horn, when suddenly, he was there.

He was standing beside a horse all painted up with swirls and stripes and there were a lot of other people around him. I recognised his father standing straight and proud beside his own horse. He had three feathers in his hair, one of them with a chunk out out, and you'd think he was carved out of the hill himself, he was that still-looking, and calm. About a dozen other men were standing with him, all of them looking and listening intently, all of them naked from the waist up and wearing a quiver with about twenty arrows. Behind them some women were standing together, holding spare horses and not talking much but looking solemn and a bit scared.

Long Horn gave me a look from his long black eyes and went back to watching and waiting. I stood next to him and thought that Long Horn was taller than me now by about half a head, and it was only a couple of days since I'd last seen him. Maybe it was the way he was standing, with every sinew strained so you could see them under his skin. It made me frightened of him for the first time.

We were peering round the bottom of the hill. It was sunny but we were in the shade and beyond the hill there was a long, wide plain with pink and white flowers and short green grass. Nobody spoke. The horses twitched. A fly settled on my cheek, tickling, and I didn't dare to brush it off.

Then suddenly there was a sound. And the waiting men got stiller and straighter. A muscle tightened in Long Horn's face. The sound was faint, then louder, then louder than ever until at last there was a roaring noise and the ground shook and you could hear a thump like a pain in your head.

When it got to its loudest Long Horn's father gave a silent sweep of his hand. After that I was up behind Long Horn surging forwards in the middle of the twelve tall men.

Long Horn's reins were tucked into his trousers so both his hands were waving free and I could feel him start to control the horse just by the pressure of his knees. We were galloping madly round the base of the hill with the sky and the grass just a blur going past when suddenly there were the buffalo.

They were like a grey sea heaving in a cloud of dust and spray. They were like paintings you saw on cavemen walls.

Long Horn yelled and wheeled us round so we were galloping away from the other men and going towards the buffalo. All you could see was wild eyes flashing and heaving flanks and horns like knives. The stink of fear rose up and filled your head and choked your nose with its awful scent.

I wanted to get off. I was being thrown this way and that, falling about like a floppy doll, and the Plain was just a blur of animals thundering and pounding with their great heads down and I knew we were going to kill one of them. If I could have done I would have yelled 'Please don't,' because I belong to Greenpeace and the Nottinghamshire Wildlife Trust. But Long Horn was beyond me now, as wild and as mad as the buffalo.

I saw we were going towards one beast. A pale grey cow, not very old. She was running hard and her mouth was foaming. We were gaining on her and she knew her death would be at our hands.

Long Horn shot an arrow straight behind her running front leg.

I saw her stumble and blood burst out and Long Horn let our horse fall back and I thought he was going to let the cow go, but he took another arrow from the quiver on his back and fit it to his bow.

It was after that that the galloping horse and the running buffalo were slowed down suddenly. I could see our one cow with the arrow in her and Long Horn pulling the bowstring tight. I saw him let it fly in a slow, sure line, straight into the cow's wet flanks. I saw her go down and struggle a bit, and then stay down with her head on the grass.

The rest of the herd were thundering on and the other men were yelling at them, but where we were it was quiet and still.

Long Horn stopped his horse and we both got off. We stood by the dead cow and I thought he would whoop or yell or whip out his knife. Instead he knelt by the animal and gently touched her flank. I thought there were tears in his eyes the same as mine, but he just gazed at the animal silently and then looked up at the sky.

The clouds were still frozen and the sun was like a round, bright crown. Slowly Long Horn raised his arms and I heard him say, very loud and slow, 'O Great One, I thank you for this beast. May I live to be worthy for another day.'

Long Horn took my wrist. 'You bring me courage, my friend. Now I may hunt whenever I choose and not stay at home with the old men and girls.'

I grasped his wrist and his hand was sticky on my skin. When he took it away I could see the buffalo's blood standing out in a bright red streak. 'Magic Eyes, we are brothers, yes?' he said.

I nodded slowly and thought that maybe I should tell him my name was Geoffrey, but I didn't because I thought there might be a right time to tell him.

Long Horn turned away from me at the same time as a woman appeared. She was leading another horse by a rope. When he saw her Long Horn quickly pulled the arrows out of the buffalo. He presented one to the woman and put the other back in his quiver. After that he jumped on to his horse and pulled me up behind him. I realised it was the same horse we broke that day in the stream, only bigger and grander and more confident.

I looked back and saw that the Plain was full of women picking their way through the fallen buffalo, examining the arrows in their flesh. It made me think of those films I'd seen of women after a battle going out to find their dead. I didn't look back again.

Next we were galloping towards the hill and as we went I felt myself slip. Down and down I went, off the horse, over its slippery dark brown flanks, down and down towards the grass.

Gran was fast asleep in her chair. *The Bill* was on the television and she had her mouth open. While I watched her she woke up.

'Eh?' she said, puzzled for a bit. 'I've just been having five minutes or so. You've not been gone long, have you, me duck?'

We watched the telly, and then had some cocoa and went to bed. In bed I looked at the moon and thought I saw the buffalo running over its surface. While I watched they grew thinner and thinner. Long Horn was somewhere beside me, waiting, and I knew that he wanted me to go with him on a journey that was terrifying, to a place I didn't want to go.

Geoffrey Superhunk

We had English next day and Miss Turner said, 'Right. I hope you've all got your ads with you. We're going to read them out and I want you to tell me, what's being advertised? Who is the target audience? What use has been made of metaphor, alliteration, adjectives, etc? Don't forget you should have rewritten the ads for a different audience. Now, who's going to volunteer to go first? Don't be shy, you've all got to do it, so there's no point in any of you hanging back.'

I slumped in my chair and kept my head well down while the other kids sat there stony-faced or tipped their desks up and giggled out loud. Michelle glanced at me and pulled a face like we were in on some kind of joke together. I pulled a face back and she got out her mirror and stared at her hair then flicked a spike that had started to droop.

Finally Miss Turner said, 'Right. Well. I can see you're not in the mood today. Michelle! We'd better start with you.'

'Why me? I'm not doing anything.' She looked aggrieved and pushed her lips out.

'Precisely!' Miss Turner said smartly back. 'So let's see how you dealt with your ad.'

Michelle scowled and gave a great big sigh and fumbled around in a plastic bag. She pulled out an advert that said 'Call me!' on it, with a picture of a mobile phone.

'Who is the advert *for*, Michelle? What do you think it's trying to say?'

Michelle shrugged and flicked at her hair again and a lad from the back called out to her, 'I'll call you, right, kiddo? Any time.'

That made some other kids start to shout, 'I'll call you stupid if you like.'

'Say that again and I'll deck you, right?' Michelle made her hand into a fist so a big ring on it caught the light.

Miss Turner gave up on her and said, 'I can see you've still got some work to do. Take half a discredit and I'll come back to you soon.'

Next she went round the other kids and most of them got away with it, so when she got to me I was confident. I'd say, 'I forgot it, Miss. I'll bring it next week.' Then I'd stare her out and she'd go away and I'd have some time to think about it.

Only wouldn't you know it didn't work? Instead of letting me off she tapped her teeth and looked annoyed and then turned back round towards her desk. She fumbled about in some messed-up papers and then held a big piece of paper up and said, 'Here you are. You can do this instead.'

The paper said 'WELL-BUILT CHUNK' in huge brown letters. Under that was a picture of a salad sandwich made with great thick slices of bread, 'THE BREAD WITH MORE BODY' and there was a scattering of crumbs. Only I'd hardly got as far as that before kids were laughing and clutching each other and yelling out stuff like, 'The invisible chunk!' and 'Oy, Geoffrey, Superhunk!' and 'Geoffrey Parker, the bloke with no body!' I wanted to say something witty and smart but couldn't think of a single thing.

Suddenly I felt very tired. I wanted to will Long Horn up here and now and gallop off on his painted horse with the other kids gawping after us.

Behind me someone was saying, 'Who's an invisible music chunk?' and Michelle was telling them to belt up or else. Miss Turner was trying to quieten everyone down and I was concentrating hard.

I thought about Long Horn, but nothing happened. Then I blinked and I got this burst of light, like a star again, red and shooting silver sparks. The blood in my veins went hot and throbbed and suddenly I wasn't tired or angry or sad any more. Something had blown up all at once. Like everything that had gone on before; Mum and Dad wafting off to Africa and me having to change to this crummy school; like being on my own the way I knew I'd end up; all that suddenly came out *POW*!

'You want to watch yourselves. You want to be careful of me,' I said.

And nobody said, 'Ooh, Geoffrey. Listen to him!'

Instead they looked at me and fidgeted and out of the corner of my eye I could see Long Horn on the Plain.

Miss Turner coughed and said, 'Now everyone, try and concentrate,' and I was back inside my own skin, only straighter and harder. It lasted for almost the rest of the day. On the way home some girl came up and said, 'Show us your muscles Geoffrey-oh,' and Michelle arrived out of nowhere special and grabbed her arm and gave her a shove.

I started to walk off down the road, and Michelle ran after me, shouting out, 'Oy! Geoffrey! Wait a mo! You're not safe out, I'll walk you home!'

I reckoned it was another of her stupid jokes so I shrugged and ignored her and I heard her say, 'Well, blow you then. See if I care.'

After that I was just about back to myself. And I'd still got the cringe-making advert to do.

I went round the back through Gran's little garden. The garden was still full of nasturtiums and marigolds and plants that looked like little red spikes. All through summer Gran worked on it, even when her back was bad. 'I like a bit of colour,' she'd say. 'Give us a hand with this trowel,

Geoffrey. That there weed's got the better of me.'

Some of the plants were going black now with the first frost on them and when I went in Gran was looking upset.

'Are you all right?' I asked, alarmed.

'I'm all right,' she said, dead quiet. 'It's Mr O'Keef, love. I'm afraid he's gone.'

'Eh?' I said, puzzled. 'Gone where? In a home? Or have his relatives finally come?'

'Don't be silly, Geoffrey. Poor Mr O'Keef died today. *Now* I except his children will come. There'll be the house to sort out and the will and that. Oh, Geoffrey, it's sad, I know, but he *was* eighty-two.'

I opened my mouth to say something and then closed it again. Because I knew for a fact that Gran was seventy-three and I didn't think she realised how old she was. She even called other people old fizz-gigs, but how much longer could she go on? All at once I felt very cold.

'You won't have to take his dinners round now,' I said, meaning that it would save her legs, especially now she was getting on.

Gran shot me a look like she was really upset and said, 'That's not a right way of thinking, Geoffrey.'

After that she bustled off to the kitchen and I heard her banging plates about and tea was sausages that she'd burnt and some chips she did on a tray in the oven.

Gran didn't want to dance that night. 'It's not respectful,' she said. She was sitting on her chair again, knitting me another hat from scraps of wool left from something else. After a while she looked up and said, 'Come here and let me measure you, love.'

I knelt down beside her on the floor and she wrapped some wool around my head and then said, still holding on so my face was clutched in her two freckled hands, '*I'm* not going anywhere, Geoffrey, love. So don't go worrying yourself about me.'

Next day I woke up yelling and seeing Mum and Dad's faces, which was weird because I'd stopped seeing them properly yonks ago. But there they were, clear and bright and unsmiling. Almost as soon as I saw them they disappeared.

Suddenly I was back at the start when Gran said I'd to go and live with her. We'd left the house and I'd switched schools and even the furniture I knew had gone. But we went on having tea and washing up, watching the telly and going for walks . . . Everything was as awful as it could be and yet so ordinary.

'Geoffrey! Geoffrey! Time to get up. Don't you dare go back to sleep.'

I went downstairs and Gran was on the phone saying, 'Yes. Yes. You're right, my dear, not chrysanths, they wouldn't suit. Mr O'Keef liked irises.'

When she came into the kitchen Gran looked at me and

said, 'You getting those bad dreams again? I thought I heard you but I was stuck on the phone – why do folks ring before half-past eight?'

I shrugged and ate some toast she'd made. We had games today and I knew that even with my best shorts on I'd get laughed at and called the invisible chunk. I mooched off out and the sky was huge like the sky on the Plain, high and clear and brilliantly blue. I expected I was going to school but then found that my feet had set off the other way, down the canal with its scruffy tow-path and geezers sitting under green umbrellas.

Apart from the traffic and the slop of the water it was dead quiet and still. You could see buses whizzing past on the viaduct and the tops of heads nodding, and nothing else. When I'd walked far enough I sat on a bench and decided that I'd come here to think.

I was back in bed again just after the yell and I'd got this picture of Mum and Dad; just their backs getting smaller and smaller and me standing where they'd left me. Gran's arm was round me and before that I'd seen her cry. Not great sobs like you can hear, but two tears falling and shattering into sparks.

'Don't worry, love, you'll see them again.'

We went to Gran's house and after that I got this blur where Mum and Dad's faces should be. I could hear them saying stuff like, 'Geoffrey, come and look at this, will you?'

And I could see them showing me Orion, the fuzzy nebula where stars are forming like a white curtain against the sky. I could feel Dad's arm round me. It was April and nearly too light and you could smell hyacinths in the garden. After we'd looked we stayed where we were, not doing anything, just sniffing the garden and being safe and all right with each other. And maybe that's why I forget things, because we never did anything that great or thrilling but just everyday stuff you don't remember.

Only then I remembered something else. Mum saying, 'You'll be having a brother soon, Geoffrey. Will you like that, d'you think? Or will you be cross?'

Mum was wearing a pink dress and open work sandals that rasped on the dry grass. When she put her head back and shaded her eyes you could see the sun shining through her hair, making it turn red and gold. She looked happy.

'I expect I'll like it,' I said cautiously.

'Oh, Geoffrey!' Mum ruffled my hair and laughed out loud. 'Never a one to say anything rash!'

Had I disappointed her? Should I have said what I really felt? Thrilled, delighted. Astonished like when you first see a meteor showering in November. Beautiful and amazing. I wanted a brother to tell things to and look after. But I never went and said it out loud.

And I never got to see my brother. After Mum and Dad left I thought about him a lot. What was he like? Did he know about me? But there was nothing afterwards to tell me anything.

Gran said later, 'Listen, Geoffrey, they didn't want to go, but they had to, right? Do you understand what I'm telling you? And you'll be OK. You just need time.'

'Got the time, mate?'

'Half-past ten.'

A bloke in front of me nodded briefly and turned off up the scruffy path. Then he stopped and said back over his shoulder, 'You want to watch it, son, there's a copper up there. I should scarper sharpish if I were you.'

For the rest of the day I just skulked around, kicking stones in the oily water and lurking under grey brick tunnels.

Later I had to lie to Gran. 'School was OK. Yeah. You know. Could have been much worse, I suppose.'

'Well, at least you kept yourself clean today. Washing! I've never known the like. I don't know what you get up to, Geoffrey. What must the other lads' mums think?'

After tea Gran said, 'Life has to go on; or where should we be? Answer me that if you can, Geoffrey.'

She meant it was OK for us to dance in spite of Mr O'Keef and she put *Hey Mr Tambourine Man* on and we did a slowish quick-step to it and Gran said, 'You'd better put your best trousers on soon and I'll have a shufty at how they look. We can't have you busting out of them before we've had the Gala Night.'

When we finished dancing we watched TV and it was a programme about elephants in the wild. You could see the elephants like big grey ships sailing across the African plain. One of them was trumpeting up to the sky. A great stark noise that went through your head, almost as if you were sitting back and hearing yourself crying out loud. At the end of the programme Gran glanced at me and said, 'OK, Geoffrey?' and touched my knee, like she knew I'd been looking for Mum and Dad somewhere among those elephants.

Later on I went upstairs and looked out of the window. Betelgeuse shouldn't have been there but it was. There was this small glow like a tiny fire in the sky which made me think of Long Horn. About what I would do if he went away. Because Long Horn was a kind of courage when I needed it. Without him there was only Gran and how much longer could she go on?

The Awaited Star

I woke up the next day with the idea that Long Horn was holding me off and I couldn't reach him if I wanted to. So I went to school feeling like I'd lost something important and I might not get it back.

And first thing off there's bullet-head Darren. Only this time he's not firing at me. He's going up to another kid, Peter Bryant who's usually quiet, and telling him he wants his snap, and following it up with a butt to the head.

I was standing watching them along with some other kids and being glad that it wasn't me. I was curious to see what Peter would do and it would have been OK if he hadn't looked at me. But he slowly turned his head round towards me and by the time I'd clocked him it was too late, because looking at Peter was like looking at myself.

Next thing, I'd said, 'Get your own snap, why don't you? Push off now and leave him alone.'

After that there was this tiny gap while Darren tried to take it all in. Then a girl said, 'Oh, Geoffrey! You're so masterful!' in a silly, jokey voice.

Darren turned round and butted me one and Peter said, 'Why'd you do that? I can handle Darren any time.' He went swaggering off and Darren came up and tried to butt me again where I was lying down until Michelle came along and hauled him off.

After that we had a History lesson with Miss Taylor who's one of the better ones. When we got in the room Mozart was playing again. I recognised the middle bit from a flute concerto, where the music goes soft and velvety, just as if you're stroking a cat. Only Miss Taylor's got the nous to keep quiet. She acts as if the music's not playing. Most of the kids start to settle down. Even Darren was just sitting quiet, like the black pit that lived between his ears had suddenly gone spaced-out and blank.

But at break time Darren came barrelling over towards me again and said, 'Hey-up, prat-face. I reckon you've not had enough of this.' He gave me a wallop that set the blood running.

Michelle Morgan said, 'Stop it, dick head.' She kicked him with her great black boot, then turned round to me and said, 'Don't you ever learn?'

A kid said, 'Blimey! Look at that! I reckon as our Michelle's in love!'

Michelle flashed her ring and said, 'Sod off!' in a bored, to-hell-with-you sort of voice. Then she hung around me for the rest of the break, not bothering to try and say anything else.

At home time I'd got blood down my shirt and I didn't feel like going to Gran's. I wanted to see Long Horn again. I wasn't even looking at the sky because of the rain and the low grey clouds. But then I did look up and I saw this star shining over Green's Mill in the rain. The shine was like a ring of sparks, not flashing, but hanging there for me to see. It wasn't Betelgeuse or any other star I knew. What I did know was that it was some kind of sign, like Long Horn was telling me he couldn't see me yet but he was still there for me, waiting.

I got back home feeling not too bad. Gran was wearing her best go-to-meeting clothes, a navy blue blouse and a pleated skirt and hat and a brooch made out of pearls at her throat.

'We sent Mr O'Keef back home today.' She took off her hat and patted her hair to settle it down. 'It was a lovely do. Quiet, but nice. That daughter of his came and we chatted and that but I'd don't reckon as how I'll see her again.'

Gran shook her head and looked upset so I said straight away to cheer her up, 'D'you want a quick dance, Gran? We've nearly got it now.'

She didn't say yes, but she smiled a bit, so I put some

music on and later Gran said, 'You're a lovely mover, you are, Geoffrey. Some girl who likes dancing will appreciate that. Now, we'll have a go at that natural weave: right hip to right hip. Keep on me toes when it comes to the "quick". Reverse. Turn on the spot. Then turn back again into the weave.'

We danced out of the room and into the hall while Gran shouted at me, 'That's *feather*, Geoffrey, not hop and skip, and *right* foot diagonal, slow, quick-quick.'

When we got in the hall the doorbell rang and Gran said, 'Now who can that be at this time of day?' And she looked alarmed like she always does when something happens she hasn't planned.

It was Ivy. 'I hope I'm not interrupting you? Only I was just passing by and I thought I'd drop in.'

Gran knew this was not quite true but relaxed her face into a very kind smile. 'It's nice to see you, love,' she said. 'I was just having a dance with Geoffrey here.'

In the background the music was still playing on and Ivy tilted her head and looked a bit sad, and the next thing is I'm saying to her, 'Would you like to dance, Ivy? I'm not too bad.'

Ivy put her bag down and looked at Gran while she took her coat off very fast, and Gran nodded and said, 'You do that, love, while I go and put the kettle on.'

Dancing with Ivy was different from dancing with Gran. It was like dancing with a small, thin bird that smelt of violets. While she danced Ivy hummed a bit and occasionally sang a few of the words. 'You're very neat, Geoffrey,' she said.

After that the doorbell rang again and this time it was Hilda from down the road. 'I didn't know you had company,' she said. 'I don't want to interrupt anything.'

Ivy said, 'We're just having a bit of a dance, Hilda.'

Hilda said, 'Well, I can see that. I like a bit a dance myself.'

And that's when Gran came in and said, 'Our Geoffrey'll give you a dance, Hilda. Let me just change the record, my duck.'

So I danced the Monet Waltz with Hilda and then the Cha-cha-cha with Gran and then the Foxtrot with Ivy again. After that everyone danced with everyone else and Gran poured the tea and mopped her face and said, 'Mr O'Keef would have enjoyed that, he was a nifty dancer in his time.'

And instead of being sad about Mr O'Keef we all drank tea and ate some crumpets that Gran had got and talked about the Gala Night.

'I shall wear me pink,' Ivy said, happily. 'With them silver shoes and me velvet rose.'

'I've got this dress I've been saving,' said Hilda. 'Bought it in Eastbourne last July. It hangs right, you know? It holds me in. And the skirt's got that bit of flare in it.'

Later on I was sitting on my bed just hanging loose when I suddenly saw Mum and Dad again. They weren't in Africa, they were in the back garden of our old home and Dad had drunk a lot of wine. He was singing, 'You're the best thing that ever happened to me,' while Mum looked embarrassed and tried not to laugh. Then she grabbed hold of me and of Dad's hand and said, 'We're the best thing that ever happened to each other.'

I think Dad fell down after that, but anyway, when I'd remembered it I saw them fade, very slowly, like they definitely didn't want to go.

After that I looked out the window and there were no stars in the sky, but I knew even so that Long Horn was there. I could feel him wanting me with him but holding back, as if he was using all his willpower for some strange reason to deliberately try and keep me away.

I woke up the next morning feeling like I hadn't slept, even though I knew that I had. I had a look at my English homework. 'WELL-BUILT CHUNK. THE BREAD WITH MORE BODY.' Who could I rewrite the advert for?

Bullet-head Darren's face cropped up. After that it was easy. I rewrote it to read 'BUY CHUMP!!' followed by a picture of two slices of bread being held apart by a prehistoric bloke with lots of hair. Underneath that I put 'THE BREAD WITH MORE BODY BUT NO BRAINS.' I was quite chuffed with that. I even got my pencils out and coloured the man in and put sweat marks flying off his face and a beard and gappy teeth.

But when I went downstairs I felt weird again. Ravenously hungry but not able to eat. Every time I put something into my mouth this invisible force seemed to stop me.

'You'll not get fat like that Geoffrey. You going down with something, my lad? Or are you just having one of your fads?' Gran was toasting bread at the electric fire because the toaster wasn't working again. Her face was shiny and she'd red striped socks on over her tights but her eyes were bright and sharp as knives.

'Just don't feel like it today.'

'You can't go off on an empty stomach. Drink this if you don't want to eat your toast.'

Gran whipped up an egg in a glass of milk and stood over me while I drank it down. But drinking it made my head go strange, as if some voice I couldn't quite hear was shouting at me to make me stop.

When I got to school Miss Turner was saying, 'Where did you get to the other day? I haven't got a form or a note anywhere. And you were missing for a whole day, Geoffrey. What have you got to say for yourself?'

I shrugged and said nothing while I wiped my specs, mainly because there was nothing to say and Miss Turner waited, tapping her nails and finally said impatiently, 'Well. You'd better go and see the Head. Straight after we've had Assembly.'

In Assembly we had to sit and clap at girls who'd scored goals in the netball team, and listen while Mr Marsden said, 'Lavatories! Cigarettes have been found clogging the bowls. Cigarettes can kill you! They're bad for your health! Cigarettes are not allowed in school!'

He went on like that while we all sat, bored. He finished up giving certificates out to some lads who'd done community work. I went to his room and stood outside with some other bad kids. One of them looked at me and blew a smoke ring and said, 'Jeez-*us*! Will you look at that! Is it cool or what? You tell me.' He went in next and crushed out his fag, and after that I had to go in. Mr Marsden was busy signing some papers and didn't look up immediately, but after a while he put his pen down and sighed and tipped his chair back a bit.

'It's Geoffrey, isn't it?' he said. 'Do you want to say anything, Geoffrey?'

And I nearly did. I don't mean about skiving off school and that, I mean about being me, Geoffrey, what it was like. And about Gran and Long Horn and Mum and Dad. But Mr Marsden sat back in his chair looking at me expectantly. You could smell cigarettes from the last kid in and there was a pile of paper slipping off his desk and this big gap that I could fill with words.

Only I didn't because Mr Marsden got fed up with waiting and said, 'I don't think I've seen you here before.

And if there's nothing you'd like to say to me, then there's something I'd like to say to you.'

After that he went on like you might expect, telling me stuff I already knew and when I went out I felt let down. I felt I'd got *that* near to something important and then I'd let it go.

When school finished it was raining again. I decided, even though it might not work, to try and get back to Long Horn. But when I got to the factory the entrance was dark. Even though the lights were on high up inside, the star was just a faint, blurred outline on the wall.

I went in close and stared at it anyway. Then blinked to try and focus my eyes.

And immediately I was somewhere else.

I was in the dark and a wind was blowing. I was alone in some high, cold place.

I was on a bare hill-top and while I stood there light seemed suddenly to arrive. I could see peaks stretching away into the distance and then disappearing into some clouds. Long Horn wasn't there, but I was aware of someone else watching and being aware of me.

Nothing moved. The peaks grew lighter and lighter, tinged with pink, and the whole world seemed enormous. Then I heard Long Horn crying out, almost like it was me crying out in my head, like an echo of something or someone that I already knew.

'Hear, Sun; hear, Old Man; Above People, listen; Under-water People, listen. Hear my cry sent to You. This Your son seeks Your aid. Hear me, Sun; hear me, Moon; Hear me, Old People. Listen to me. I plead with You.'

The voice was high and thin and fanned out round the mountain peaks until it faded slowly and silence came when I began to dance a slow kind of shuffle: shuffle, bump, shuffle, bump, with my feet banging down on the ground, my arms raised up to the sky and calling again, 'Hear me, People. This is Your son.'

Even when I was dead tired I had to go on dancing and calling out, 'Hear me; hear me; come to my aid.'

But no one answered and I could hear the voice in my head, light and floaty, carried up the mountains by the cold breeze while hunger clawed at my stomach and my arms and legs were shaking with pain. I lay down on the bare hill looking at the sky and instead of being scared I was peaceful in a way I hadn't been, not once, not since Mum and Dad went away. I gave a big sigh and a strange voice boomed out.

'Why do you lie down, my son? Why do you not seek the Power?'

The unseen stranger was standing there, sent by the tribe to watch over me. He was tall and thin with long grey hair. He wore a buffalo cloak and carried a stick. Bears' teeth were in a yellow row fastened round his wrinkled neck and he wore three tall feathers on the crown of his head.

When he spoke I was up again without even knowing how it happened. I was dancing and calling out some more, 'Come, Sun; come, Underwater People; come, Above People: listen to me and help me now.'

But nothing happened again. Just ideas came and went in my head until the sun began to drop and the coldness made me fall to the ground.

It was then another star appeared. It came bounding through the dark sky, nearer and nearer, until you could see sparks whizzing off it and feel the silver flare on your face. The star was like a crown of light with a red eye in the middle. It was the star I knew I'd been waiting for.

'My son, why do you lie here thus?'

In the star I saw a warrior, or the warrior *was* the star. He was blazing and his arms were folded and you could see muscles like oiled springs coiled tightly under the skin. Before I could answer the warrior sat down. A pipe appeared in his right hand and he smoked it slowly, puffed out the smoke and through it said, 'You called to me and I have come to you. I will give you my Power. From henceforth you must be brave and strong. But you must take my name and never change it. Remember this when you pray to me, and when you pray, I will give you aid.'

He puffed out another cloud of smoke and made rippling smoke rings in the sky. When the smoke rings cleared the warrior was gone and I was back in my own Geoffrey skin.

But I knew now that I *had* got Power and could do any stuff I wanted to.

I lay still on the ground and Long Horn called out, 'Magic Eyes! Magic Eyes! Do you hear me?'

He was in front of me and he was looking tired. His body seemed thinner but he was standing up straight and his eyes had this kind of light in them. He was wearing a shirt made out of fine buffalo skin and I knew it was the buffalo we'd killed. Moons and stars were painted on it, but none of them were as bright as Long Horn's face.

'My friend, you bring me great good fortune. Today I am full of special Power. You bring me the sign to tell me so: from now on I will be called Blazing Star. That is my name. It is meant for me. It is the proper name for a man, my friend.'

Very slowly I got to my feet. I was under the arch of faded stars, looking at Blazing Star and knowing I'd never be like him, not if I lived for a thousand years.

'How did I come here?' I asked, stupidly.

And Blazing Star walked over towards me. You could see him shimmering faintly in the hollow light and for a moment I thought he was going to disappear without answering. But then he took hold of my wrist again and I got this pulse of something. Not power, but a kind of strength I didn't think I'd ever had before.

'You came because you wanted to,' he said.

After that the pressure of his hand got lighter. The stars

came out in the sky again and when I looked up they swooped down to meet me. I was moving along in this nest of stars and I was seeing the old man with his buffalo robe; I was dancing and dancing and couldn't stop; I was hungry and cold and wishing for food.

And then suddenly I was on Hockley Lane walking slowly towards Gran's house.

Doubt

'Shtand shtill while I pin you up.'

It was the next night and Gran had pins in her mouth while she fiddled around with my best trousers so they'd be OK to wear on Gala Night.

'Clothes!' Gran had said earlier, 'I can hardly keep you decently clad. You grow that much, I don't know. And feet! I could get two of mine in one of your shoes!'

Gran was proud of her feet in spite of their corns and a bunion coming. 'Look at that arch, Geoffrey,' she'd say, sticking out her foot. 'That's a dancer's foot, that is, you mark my words.'

Now Gran was smacking my legs and moaning at me because I couldn't keep still. 'And what was that on your best school shirt? Blood, that's what! Did you have a nose bleed? You should carry that key to put down your back. I used to get nose bleeds when I was your age. It sort of runs in the family.'

'It wasn't a nose bleed. I was in a fight.'

'You what?' Gran spit the pins out of her mouth and sat on her heels and looked at me.

And I said again, quite calmly, 'I was in a fight. It's what you do at that stupid school.'

'Well!' Gran went pink. 'I've never heard the like!'

'It happens.' I shrugged as if I didn't care. I didn't care that much.

'But what were you fighting *about*?' Gran asked.

I thought of telling her what went on, but I didn't in case it made her upset.

'It was nothing much,' I said, 'Just a spat. Can't even remember what about. It happened and then it was over, right?'

'No, it's not right, Geoffrey.' Gran stood up, creaking, with the pins in her hand and said, 'Now tell me, is someone bullying you? Because they've got a policy at that school. It said so in the hand-out I read. "Bullying won't be tolerated." That's what it said, as clear as clear.'

'I'm not being bullied, it just happened.'

'Well then, Geoffrey.' Gran looked stern. 'Are *you* the bully? Is that the truth?'

'No!'

'I don't like this, Geoffrey. You're not telling the truth. And if you *are* going round thumping other kids, which I doubt because I know you too well, then I want to know all about it now. Because,' said Gran, getting into her flow the way Mum used to when she was het-up, 'I've brought you up to be thoughtful and kind. I'd expect you to set an example at school.'

'Yeah, yeah.'

'Right then, Geoffrey, I shall say no more. But I shall keep a lookout to see what's what, and if there's any more trouble I shall go up to school.'

'You can't do that! I'd not live it down! Nothing happened, believe me, Gran!'

But I was wasting my breath because Gran folded her lips together and looked stern again. It's like that time a dog crapped outside our house and Gran parcelled it up very neat and clean and went round and knocked on the owner's door. She gave them the parcel and said, 'I think this is yours. Don't let me find it on my step again.'

When Gran finished talking I kept quiet while she sewed my trousers with a sharp snap of thread. While she was doing it, Ivy came.

'Just passing by,' she said, beaming. 'No music tonight? Well, I am surprised.'

'We're getting our Geoffrey kitted out. Grow! He's like a blinking tree.'

'My Keith used to grow like that. And food! I wouldn't want the feeding of him again.'

'Aye, well. Our Geoffrey's got a good appetite. Go and slip

into these will you, love? While I go and put the kettle on.'

I went upstairs and got into the trousers and when I came down they both looked up and smiled.

Ivy put a hand to her chin. 'He's a fine-looking lad,' she said to Gran.

And Gran harrumphed and looked pleased but all she said was, 'Handsome is as handsome does. It's the way he behaves as counts the most.'

'Well. He'll make hearts flutter in a few years' time. And those specs are kind of distinguished looking.'

They got me to turn round this way and that while Ivy said, 'Not a white shirt, I think. Dark blue, maybe. Or even red.'

'Just what I was thinking,' said Gran, 'and not a dickie, but an open neck.'

They nattered some more while I went back upstairs and got into my scruffy jeans. I put Sibelius's *Finlandia* on dead loud and then leaned my elbows on the window-sill. It was dark and the moon was up and it was so big and bright I thought I could see the craters on it, Tycho and Clavius, like swollen gaps with the light shining through. Then out of the corner of my eye I saw the For Sale sign on Mr O'Keef's front gate. Suddenly, I was back in the street where I used to live. Some men were nailing up a For Sale sign in our front garden and the sound of it made me think I'd never, ever go back. It was the last week of the holidays and summer was nearly over and it was raining. Rain dripped off the big trees in the road and you could hear it rushing down the gutters, but you could still smell roses.

The school I used to go to was small and people talked to you like you were OK. You could listen to music apart from the Back Street Boys and hip-hop and talk about it without someone making out you were weird. They even liked you to learn stuff. I learned Latin and Algebra and this poem about the stars being seared on the sky that's locked in my brain like it's grafted on:

> *A radiant welt*
> *Sears the firmament's*
> *Black heart*
> *For ever*
> *Marked with glory*

Surely I didn't pretend all *that*? *One Wheel On My Wagon* blasted through the ceiling and I closed the curtains and went downstairs. Gran and Ivy were dancing together, side-stepping and going hand-in-hand and clapping and laughing and shouting 'Hi!'

'Geoffrey!' Gran said, looking round. 'D'you want to dance or are you doing something?'

'I'm busy tonight,' I said, lying and trying not to notice Ivy's drooping face.

Only I didn't feel like dancing then. It's like being with Blazing Star had made me so I didn't know what was what any more. I mean, supposing I wasn't actually real, but just a spirit who thought he was?

Or supposing (and this is what scared me most) that my only purpose for existing at all was to be called up now and then by Blazing Star?

But I was real enough at school. Miss Turner said, 'We'll finish off our adverts today. Geoffrey, I think we'll start with you.'

I held up my ad for the class to see and the background rumble turned into voices shouting, 'Oy, Geoffrey, what's your beef?' and 'That's Granny's boy, not granary!'

'What did you get from the advert, Geoffrey? Is there any alliteration or pun?'

Miss Turner waited with her head cocked to one side ignoring the class and tapping her ruler on her skirt.

'It's got two b's at the end,' I said, 'so I s'ppose that might be alliterative. And chunk and body could be called puns.'

'Well done, Geoffrey. And who do you think the advert's for?'

Miss Turner had to talk louder then because the other kids were still shouting out, 'Alliterative! Ooh, Geoffrey, that's a big word for you to say!'

The loudest voice was Peter Bryant's. He was sitting at the

back tipping his chair up and mouthing off and making sure I knew he was one of the in-guys now and didn't want to get confused with me.

I shrugged and put the advert down and said, 'I expect it's for the folks who like to be healthy. It's to get them to eat that particular bread.'

'And have you rewritten it for a different audience?'

'Yeah.' Why did it not seem so funny now?

'Well, Geoffrey?'

The bloke in the sandwich looked even more like Darren than I remembered, except for the stubble on his chin.

'Read it out, Geoffrey.'

I cleared my throat and read 'BUY CHUMP! THE BREAD WITH MORE BODY BUT NO BRAIN' and then put it down on my desk very fast.

A few kids giggled and Miss Turner looked uncertain and said, 'Well, it's unusual, Geoffrey, I'll give you that. Who do you think the advert's for?'

I shrugged again and Miss Turner reached across my desk and picked up the ad to show the class.

That's when they all started laughing out loud. They laughed and shoved each other and said, 'Oy, that's Darren, that is, Miss! He's the filling in the middle, he is! The beef with no brain! That's him all right. Here, Darren, cop a look at this!'

To begin with I thought I was going to get off, mainly

because Darren didn't catch on. He thought they were laughing *with* him, right? And he laughed back and banged dead loud on his desk until suddenly you saw his brain give a click. His face went black and his eyes sunk in and he grabbed the advert off a kid and looked at it and ripped it up.

I was looking at Miss Turner who was going red but I could see Darren out of the corner of my eye. I saw his head turn very slowly in my direction.

Miss Turner said, 'No need for that, Darren. Pick up the pieces. Thanks for your contribution, Geoffrey.'

At home time I could see some kids standing by the cycle sheds mucking about. Michelle was with them, smoking a fag, and Peter Bryant with his hands in his pockets, laughing but looking embarrassed as well. When I got up close Michelle shouted out, 'Watch it, Geoffrey, over there.' I turned round to look just as Darren steamed out from the dark space between the shed and the wall. He'd his fists bunched up and his head tucked down and I knew as he'd get me for good this time.

I'm looking at Darren but it's like he's not there. I can see him coming up towards me fast and this voice in my head says 'step aside.' So I side-step quite neatly and Darren goes past, then he shakes his head and comes back at me, and this voice says, 'Trip him up now.'

When Darren came up I stuck out my foot and he

lurched for a moment and then went down and I could have clocked him before he got up.

But I didn't. Instead I slowly put my fist down. Behind me I could hear Michelle saying in a disappointed voice, 'Why didn't you sock 'im one, Geoffrey?'

Then Darren got up and he was socking *me* and saying, 'What's a chump, prat, anyway?' And I went down with these stars in my head. The stars were like a meteor falling. They were showering down in total silence, slowly, like a cosmic display set up on purpose just for me. When the meteor finished it went dark and still. Then out of the darkness this light came on, dazzling and sparking with a deep red eye. For a moment it looked at me, steady and unblinking. Then it switched off suddenly and blackness came and I was lying exactly where Darren put me, conked out on the cold, hard ground.

The Wolf

There was blood on my shirt again when I got home and I went upstairs before Gran could see. I rinsed the blood off and hung the shirt over the radiator and put my jeans on and went downstairs. Gran was sitting at the kitchen table. She was dipping digestive biscuits in a mug of tea and then eating the soggy bit before it dropped off.

'Me teeth are playing up today, Geoffrey. You just be glad you've got all your own.'

Next to Gran's mug on the table there was a big plastic bag and in between the glugs of biscuit Gran was looking pleased with herself.

'I had a win at bingo today and I shared it with Ivy like she does with me, but there was enough left over to buy you a shirt. Have a look at it, Geoffrey, love. It's for you to wear on Gala Night.'

I opened the bag reluctantly and took this shirt out made

of some sort of crimson stuff with a double frill going down the front.

'I can't wear that!'

'You'll look a treat in it, Geoffrey! You'll look like the bloke in that whatsit film. The one who dances and gets the lass. Just put it on, love, and let's have a look.'

And here's a funny thing about Gran: she's got this eye you forget about. It only seems to work with clothes and mainly with other people, but this time it actually worked for me.

I got into the shirt and the Gala Night trousers. I had a look in my flecky mirror and gave a gasp and took a step back. The frills made me look different, taller and broader, much more like a real grown-up.

I turned about this way and that, and pranced a bit and did some steps and remembered Ivy saying, 'Those specs are kind of distinguished looking.' They were new ones with dark brown frames Gran had bought me specially for Gala Night. I adjusted them so they sat straight on my nose and then practised a smile showing all my teeth.

When I went downstairs Gran was sitting with one foot on her knee, rubbing at it with both her hands.

'Me corns are playing up again. Always look after your feet, Geoffrey.'

After she said that she glanced up. Then she slowly put her foot on the floor and to begin with she didn't say anything. She was staring at me and she put a hand up to her chest like she does when she's eaten nuts or rhubarb and it's started to disagree with her.

'You're growing up, Geoffrey,' she said in the end. 'I can see that now. You look smashing, love, but what do *you* think?'

' 'S'OK,' I said, and shrugged and scowled.

'Well, I suppose I shall have to get used to it.'

Then, 'What d'you mean " 'S'OK"?' she said. 'Anyone can see with half an eye you look smashing in that, so don't scowl at me. And all you want to make it even better is a really nice red cummerbund.'

I shrugged again and slouched away and when I got upstairs I had another look. The mirror reflected the red of the shirt, and for a second I thought I saw something else, a flash of something shiny and magnificent. An indian in the speckled glass with red stripes running across his face, raising his spear up to the sun.

For one quick beat I looked into his eyes, then I gave a blink and looked away and when I looked again there was only me.

After tea Gran sent me to Boots to get a plaster for a new corn she'd got. When I came out of the shop the streets were clear and there was this funny light like a thin red disc directly over me in the sky. It wasn't as bright as Betelgeuse, but bright enough for me to think that the eye was waiting for me to notice it. A mucky rain was falling by then and the light was fading bit by bit.

I dashed the rain from off my face, and abruptly the rain turned to bullet-like snow. The snow began falling faster and faster, clattering on me and sticking there. Through the snow I could see some trees, bending under the weight of it. Behind them the sky was dark grey and hanging, and while I looked I heard a voice.

'Magic Eyes! Magic Eyes! Is it you?'

'Where are you?' I shouted, and turned round to look. And nearly collapsed in the snow with fright.

A wolf was standing in front of me. A wolf with a full set of grinning teeth and sharp pointed ears and a long thick tail. While I looked the wolf gave a sudden jerk and the head fell back with a sickening clump and Blazing Star's thin face appeared.

'You came,' he said, and he smiled. But it was a smile to nearly break your heart because Blazing Star was dull and yellow. His face was blistered and cracked with cold and you could see the bones of his skull stand out.

'Now we go together. You and me, Magic Eyes, yes? We kill a buffalo today and save my people who starve to death.'

The snow storm in my face was like an ice-cold fire. But I went slowly up to Blazing Star and touched my cold right hand to his. Then I got under the evil dead wolf-skin and slowly we clawed our way through the woods, past a thin horse pawing for grass and a bird lying dead with its claws in the air. Past a river that was frozen over and a dead tree frozen like icicles. We got to a valley knee-deep in snow. By then the cold was in my bones and I thought we'd be found in spring, starved to death and frozen solid with the snow melting off our frozen clothes.

'Here,' I handed some chocolate to Blazing Star.

And that's when he broke my heart again, because very carefully he snapped the bar in two. With a proud look he gave me the bigger half and I knew I had to eat it.

We crouched in the snow under the skin, not speaking much because our faces hurt. We were on our bellies in the bullet-like snow when without any warning it was clear as clear. In front of us you could see buffalo standing where they'd drifted before the storm like massive, hulking, snow-covered ghosts.

One buffalo was standing apart from the rest. Its shoulders were down and it looked old, or it might have been the white snow on its coat. Slowly Blazing Star trained his arrow on it. It was in his sights and the bow was stretched when all at once I saw it look up. Its great head lifted and turned towards us and my heart gave this giant, tippling lurch, because if the buffalo saw us and stampeded the herd, it would be the end for Blazing Star.

But the buffalo put its head down again. It pawed heavily on the grass at the same time as Blazing Star loosed his arrow.

In silence we watched the arrow swoop its way over the snow with a shadow so fast you couldn't see it move. Still silent, we watched the beast fall down and its blood make a patch of red on the snow. Then the other animals began to run so the earth was full of snow flying up and straining beasts, with the snow on their pelts slipping and landing with a thud on the ground.

When they'd gone Blazing Star stayed quiet, just staring ahead. After that he raised my hand in his to the sky and shouted as loud as his weak voice could, 'Hear me, Powers of Earth and Sky. Hear me, Under and Over Men. Thank you for this the gift of life. May we live to see another spring.'

We got back to camp a long time later. By then it was nearly dark and too cold for snow. Breathing the raw air was like breathing steel and the weight of buffalo cut up in our bags was like the weight of a hundred dead men.

Nobody came out to greet us. No kids were playing and no drums beat. Only a trickle of smoke rose from a tent and there was this ery quiet, as though we were the only ones left alive. Then this figure appeared out of the night. He seized Blazing Star's hand and I could feel its pressure just as if he was holding mine.

'My son,' the figure said. 'You are in time.'

Blazing Star's father was skeleton thin. His two eyes were like black holes in a skull but you could see the look in them, steady and proud and kind. I had the idea that he was looking through Blazing Star directly at me.

The pressure on my hand got stronger after that. Up in the northern sky Pegasus reared like a great square horse, higher and higher until all you could see was the dense black night folding down like a huge thick cloak.

The cloak wrapped round me and the whirling started. I was trying to say something but didn't get the chance and maybe that was just as well because the thing I was going to say was 'Dad?'

That night I dreamed about Dad again. He was packing things up and I don't mean books and pots and pans and that. I was looking at him and bits were disappearing, first his eyes, next his hair that waved at the front, then his hands that were holding a big grey rock.

To begin with I didn't mind what I saw. 'You'll be coming back soon, won't you, Dad?' I said. That was when his smile disappeared and this coldness happened. After that I started shouting, 'Dad! Dad! You're coming back!' but he kept on going a piece at a time until there was only me left and I was crying.

'What's the matter, love? Are you having one of your dreams again?'

Gran was in my room stroking my hair. She didn't have any teeth in and it made her face look gummy and wrinkled like an old baby.

'Dunno,' I said, and humped in my pillow.

'Is it that bird again? Is that what it is?'

Gran sat on the bed and put a hand on her back while I tried not to answer in case it made what I'd seen more real.

'Is it your mum and dad, Geoffrey? Because it's OK to tell me if it is.'

'It's not anything,' I said. 'Nothing to bother about, anyway.'

Gran lifted her hair-net and tucked some hair in. 'Well then,' she said, 'I shall stay here and keep you company, love. Just in case the nothing comes back.'

She settled herself on the end of the bed and the good thing was she seemed happy about it. The bad thing was, I was happy, too.

The bird comes in the night. It's a great black hawk that swoops through the sky getting bigger and bigger and blacker and lower. Then the hawk goes bang! and disappears and you think you might have disappeared with it but you wake up yelling and know you haven't.

I went to sleep with Gran still there and woke up in the morning alone. Gran was busy making some tea when I came downstairs. All she said was, 'Eat your breakfast, Geoffrey, and look sharp. And don't forget we'll be dancing later, so save some energy up for me.'

At school I ignored kids saying, 'Make my day, chunk.' At break we all had to go outside, even though rain was coming on and it was cold enough to see your breath. I was leaning on a wall with my hands in my pockets when Michelle came strolling up. For a moment she stood there, eyeing me, so I could see the stud in her nose and these rings on her hands with black painted nails. Her hair stood up in bright red spikes and while I tried not to look like I'd noticed it, she dove in a pocket and pulled something out.

'Fag?' she said.

She shoved the packet over towards me and I was that flabbergasted my jaw dropped down.

'What?' I said.

'You know. A fag. Like you smoke.'

'No thank you,' I replied very primly, as if I was telling Gran off about bingo. 'Smoking's really bad for your health.'

After that I reckon *her* jaw dropped because she stood there with the fags in her hand and the breeze waving the funny fringe thing that hung down under her black leather sleeve.

But then this smile came over her face. By then I'd my arms folded over my chest and this black scowl starting because I'd got her game sussed; she was going to get me in trouble and I wasn't going to fall for that.

When she'd finished smiling she let our this laugh '*Ha*!' that was more like a cackle than a real laugh and it made some of the other kids look our way. Then she said, 'You're something *else*. You know that, Geoffrey? I mean, you're original, aren't you? You just don't *care*.'

She put the fags back in her pocket and said, 'I'll be seeing you later, Geoffrey. Ciao.'

After that nobody bothered me any more. At home time I was starting to go up by the sheds when I saw Michelle leaning on the fence. She was blowing smoke rings and not looking my way, so I nipped off sharpish down the other path and got home later than I should have done because the other path was the long way round.

Gran was out, so I went upstairs and changed into my scruffy jeans. I looked out of the window. You couldn't see Jupiter or the moon but the clouds were swirling and making a shape. While I watched the shape grew bigger and darker. It loomed in the sky like a giant hawk flapping silently nearer and nearer.

That's when my head began to sing and this eery noise came, *Boom*! *Crash*! Next thing my head's banged against the glass and I'm shouting at it, 'Leave me alone!'

'Geoffrey! Geoffrey! Are you all right?'

I heard Gran shouting from downstairs just as the hawk made a silent dive and disappeared back inside its dream life.

'Yeah,' I said, but I stayed where I was and Gran said,

'I've been at the Mothers' Union, love. The vicar doesn't dare stick his nose in there and I've brought a cake back if you fancy it.'

Gran was taking her hat off in the hall and putting it on a special peg. When I went down she put her arm through mine and said, 'I was lucky to get that cake, you know. Eat! They're like gannets for all they're so old.'

After tea she put a record on and we did a saunter to get warmed up. To begin with Gran danced in her pom-pom slippers so she seemed smaller than usual, and more clumsy, and I fretted again in case she died.

'Gran, are you feeling OK?'

Gran snorted. 'What sort of question is that, Geoffrey? Of course I'm OK. I don't know. I just haven't got my lipstick on.'

When we'd done the saunter she went upstairs and came down wearing her dancing shoes. 'Now then, love. Let's give it our best. I reckon we could win that blinking spot prize.'

She put *Unforgettable* on and we waited two beats and then started off with Gran giving all the instructions out.

'Wonderful, Geoffrey,' she said halfway through. 'Your feathering's come on a real treat but you want to watch yourself in the weave.'

We finished the practice quite late on and Gran sat in a chair to get her puff. 'Only a few days to go,' she said. 'There'll be vol-au-vents, Geoffrey, and prawn cocktails, and a choice of salmon or sirloin of beef with a pudding to follow, trifle, I expect. The spot prize is usually a big box of chocs and there's a raffle with wine to win, and ladies' tights.'

'Yeah,' I said, and worried some more because most stuff's better imagining it and I didn't want Gran to feel let down.

When I'd had my cocoa I went upstairs and looked in the speckly mirror again. And maybe it was me imagining things, or maybe I was standing straighter than usual, because I definitely thought I looked taller and broader. But when I tried to sleep I was still dead scared in case the nightmare hawk came again.

I reckoned it was connected with Blazing Star.

The Black Hole

Nobody came near me at school the next day. Even Darren seemed to have got called off. In History Miss Taylor was playing Mozart again. This time it was the middle bit from the *Sinfonia Concertante*, but I never said anything, I just watched the other kids settle down with these puzzled looks, like they knew they were doing something weird but couldn't quite work out what it was.

At dinner time Michelle sauntered up. She was chewing gum and said, 'Want a bit? Or will it make you poorly, Geoffrey, dear?'

I shrugged and took some and Michelle leaned back against the wall and I could see the other kids wondering what was up. For a minute or two neither of us spoke, then Michelle pulled a string of gum from her mouth and very slowly sucked it back in.

'Wotchyou do at night?' she said.

I shrugged again and stayed silent and Michelle blew a bubble that was large and grey and then snapped it to pieces with her tongue.

'D'you do stuff with your gran?' she asked.

'Might do,' I said, scowling at her.

'*What* d'you do?' she asked again.

'We dance,' I said, and glanced away because I didn't want to see what her face looked like after I'd said that.

'You're kidding! What – you mean disco stuff? Like how old is your gran, anyway?'

'What's it to you?' I said, fed up.

Michelle stopped her chewing and looked surprised and said, 'Nothing much. Just, I reckon it's cool to dance with your gran. I haven't got one. So what dance d'you do?'

And even though I knew what would happen next and could hear the stick I'd get inside my head, I told her, because not telling her would make me feel like I was ashamed of Gran.

Afterwards Michelle stared at me with her mouth wide open so you could see the wodge of gum inside. Then she threw back her head and gave a laugh like the one she gave the day before, only longer and louder and harsher than that.

When she'd finished her laugh she slapped my shoulder, still with her face all red and creased and said, 'You're barmy, Geoffrey. You're a raving nutter. But you're funny, you know? I mean, you're unique. So will you teach me to do the

Foxtrot, then? It'd be kinda cool, you know, to do that. Maybe your gran could teach me the steps?'

That's when I got this image of Michelle with her black painted fingernails and glinting nose stud and her red hair standing up on top, in amongst Gran's dancing cats and flowery sofa with the antimacassar.

I didn't say anything back, mainly because I didn't know what, and in a minute Michelle wandered off and I waited for the stick to happen, but it didn't. Just, Michelle kept looking at me in class and giving this weird kind of secret smile.

After school I was starting to walk back home and I'd nearly got there when I felt something that was not a pull, exactly, but more like a sudden knowledge that you're being looked at. I glanced up at the sky but the red star wasn't there. In its place there was this tense, white moon, bigger and more glowing than usual, and the light from it was like a wave in my head that I couldn't control, swirling towards me in a great wash of light. For a second or two I stood stock still with the street and Green's Mill lit up in front of me, but then they vanished in this flash of light and abruptly, Blazing Star was there.

I was in some woods with him and there were other young men standing about. They were singing quietly and when Blazing Star saw me he carried on singing. While he sang he fingered a pipe and the skin of a small animal that was brown and cracked. Round his neck there was the skull of another animal and his face was painted with crescents and stars.

It was still dark but the moon was huge and you could tell by the quiet voices and the sharp way the bones stood out from the young men's faces that something terrifying was going to happen. Blazing Star moved silently towards me and said very softly, 'I take two horses today, Magic Eyes. Maybe three now that you are here.' After that he just stood, very tall and still, his skin gleaming in the light from the moon, and the straight white feathers stood out from his head.

Then a signal happened somewhere and the singing stopped abruptly. Blazing Star motioned me to follow him and we were moving noiselessly through the damp, cool night. When we stopped the moon was getting thinner and the sky was pale with a silvery light. You could see dew on the long grass and in front of us was a camp with pointed tents and thin brown dogs in front of then. Some of the young men began to walk slowly and carefully towards the camp. A dog begin to bark so the men threw it something and the dog shut up. The rest of us began to move silently towards them.

We were going to steal some horses. I turned round to look at Blazing Star, willing for him to turn us both back because there were only eight of us and about thirty tents.

When we were in the camp the sky turned pink all at

once with the dawn coming and I went with Blazing Star to a tent where a horse was tethered outside to a stake. It was a magnificent beast, big and white with a wild black eye rolling at us. Swiftly Blazing Star cut the rope and the horse followed him, mild as milk, to the next tent where he did the same.

By then I was that frightened my legs were scissoring and it was getting lighter all the time. In another minute the camp would be up and I thought we should go now and get somewhere safe. But Blazing Star looked at me and flashed his teeth.

He whispered, 'One for you, now, eh? Magic Eyes?'

He put this knife in my hand. The others were leading their horses away and inside a tent I heard someone cough, then the murmur of a deep, strange voice.

'Jeez!' I said, under my breath. 'Let me live to see another day.'

We were up then to the next horse. 'Quickly, my friend. Before the eye of the moon disappears.'

I put the shaking knife on the rope and the horse danced his feet a bit so you could hear. From inside the tent came another voice, lighter this time, and sounding alarmed. The horse was brilliant. He was dense, coal black with a blaze on his nose and these long thin legs like on a race horse. I wanted him, but I couldn't get the knife to go through the rope. The more I tried the worse it got and by then we were the only ones left in camp. If I could have, I would have legged it off back up the hill.

But you can't. Not with Blazing Star looking at you and expecting you to be even braver than he is. So I carried on cutting as hard as I could and suddenly the horse was free and we were leading it away with the other two, making for the edge of the camp.

A tent flap went up and a black eye looked out and suddenly there was this noise of shouting and cursing and blood-curdling yells.

After that Blazing Star was up on a horse and I was scrabbling at my horse's bare black sides and not being able to get a foot up. Blokes behind us were spilling out of tents and coming after us with long sharp knives.

'Quickly, quickly,' Blazing Star yelled. 'Don't climb, jump! Quickly, my friend!'

I reckoned I was a gonner for sure when the horse slowed down suddenly. I thought he was going to turn round and gallop off. Instead he reared up on his back legs like a magnificent, gleaming black Pegasus, so his back was closer to the ground. The rearing seemed to go on and on in perfect silence so you could see the animal's blazing pelt with the sky behind it, orange and gold. After that I was on its back and leaning forward clutching its mane, careering after Blazing Star with this raw, sick feeling still in my throat.

We went for miles with the sun behind us and when we

stopped we weren't anywhere. There was just scrub and grass and bent brown trees for as far as you could properly see, and I was stiff and aching, but calm again.

I got off the horse and rubbed his flank. My legs were shaking and the horse was flecked in white foamy sweat and blowing savagely through his nose. But he let me stroke him.

'He is yours, my friend. For ever. You see? Whenever you want him, he will be there.'

Blazing Star was still on his horse and he looked amazing; tall and proud with long flowing hair. His feathers were like a crown on his head and the stars and moons glowed red on his face.

I nearly wished a stupid wish, then; that I had my red shirt with frills on so he could see that I could look great as well. But when I looked again the thought disappeared and instead there was this terrible sadness. It came to me that Blazing Star was slowly drawing away. He was getting older and older each time we met and soon he would be too old for me.

Almost as if he read my thoughts Blazing Star reached down suddenly and touched my shoulder. 'My friend,' he said softly, 'soon we will have come as far as we can. But I will see you again, very soon, I know. Take care, my friend, and remember the horse.'

I saw the horse again the next day. It was morning and I

wasn't looking for him, but he came out of a waking dream. In the dream it had snowed and I was shovelling snow with Dad. We were doing the drive that went round our house and we could hear each other grunt. The sky was pale grey and you knew more snow might come but you felt cosy somehow, like the snow and the sky were a blanket round you and you were safe inside it.

Then Mum came out with some mugs of cocoa and slices of toast and we had this kind of picnic outside. It felt happy and safe, like nothing bad could ever happen.

I expect I was smiling in my dream when the hawk came. I was looking at the grey sky as it got nearer and nearer so you could hear its wings flapping, but the noise they made was more like an engine. When the noise was overhead it stopped, ready to make the bang. I was cowering under the bedclothes, waiting for it, but instead of the bang this horse came galloping. And maybe I sent for him. Next thing is, I'm up on the horse and we're flying and flying, I don't know where to. Then Gran called me.

'Geoffrey! Geoffrey! You'll be late for school!'

I went downstairs and said, 'What d'you want to do that for? I was all right in bed.'

Gran looked cross. Her face was pink from the stove and she said, ladling out porridge, 'That's as maybe. Now get this inside you and pipe down.'

While I was eating she said, 'It's Gala Night tomorrow,

Geoffrey. It'd be a kindness if you'd dance with Ivy – a saunter or a swing-time, perhaps – only one dance just to please her, like.'

'OK,' I muttered.

'And I got you a cummerbund yesterday. You can give it a try tonight, Geoffrey. Make sure it goes right round your waist – though there's nothing much on you, not like me.'

'You're fine, Gran, honest. You look dead great,' I said, mainly because of the note in Gran's voice, like she was really cheesed off.

'Go on with you,' Gran sounded pleased and not wanting to show it. She turned round and thwacked some more porridge out and said, 'You're a real charmer when you want to be. But remember, Geoffrey, a silver tongue is all very well as long as it doesn't hide a black heart.'

I got to school and Darren was there, standing on his own with his back to the wall and trying not to look like he minded these kids who were laughing and digging each others' ribs. I made to go past him when I heard one of them say to him, 'Fell off your bike! You ain't got one! What you telling us? You think we're daft?'

'So who went and walloped you one then, me old mate? Go on! You can tell us! We won't laugh!'

'No one, I told you. I fell off me bike.'

'Pull the other one! It's got bells on, like.'

They went on like that until we got into school and I

copped a look at Darren's face. His left eye was purple and black and red, and when he saw me looking he made a rude sign and tried to look fierce but looked stupid instead.

Nobody bothered me again all day. Even in English when Miss Turner said, 'Here's your bread homework back, Geoffrey,' all I got was somebody muttering, 'Right on, chunk,' under their breath.

I went straight home to Gran's and the phone rang when I'd got in the door. It was Brian. 'You coming round for a special do? It's Leonids. We should get a good look.'

'You're on,' I said and put the phone down and went to get changed into my jeans.

I told Gran I was going out and she said, 'Brian and his wife are good sort of folks. Now, just try this on, love, before you go.'

She took a red cummerbund out of a bag and fastened it round my waist, then stepped back and gave a great big sigh and said, 'Well, Yes. It looks a treat.' And I gave her a hug because she looked upset like she was missing me, even though I was standing there.

When Brian came he had soup down his jumper and some yellow bits that might be egg. When we got to the dome the telescope was up, and just with your eye you could see the black sky and some bright bits darting and flashing about. But when you looked through the 'scope it was something else. It was like silver rain falling up and down, then whizzing in a silver streak through the sky. It was like celestial fireworks, you could see God laughing and you felt sorry for all those people indoors watching *Coronation Street* and chewing sweets and waiting for the ten o'clock news.

I was looking at it for the second time, the radiant point in Leo like a great shaggy lion with its mane flashing sparks, when one of the stars seemed to change to red. It was silver, then red. And it stayed red. Not only red, but it stopped shooting and waited over where I was with the other stars whizzing round it. Then suddenly it was gone like a light switched off and where it had been was a big black hole, blacker than you could ever imagine, blacker than the blackest night.

Across the sky stars were still shooting and I could hear Brian going 'ooh' and 'aah', but in the place where my heart should be suddenly there was this great crushing gap that made me lean right over towards the floor and clutch myself across the chest.

'All right, son?' Brian looked concerned.

'Stitch.'

'Fair enough.' Brian looked away.

After that the pain quietened down a bit and I hung around until it was time to go home, then asked Brian to drop me at the fish 'n' chip shop.

'Gives you an appetite, star-gazing does.'

Brian grinned in the dark when I opened the door and I

gave him a nod and got out the car. But I didn't go to the fish 'n' chip shop. Instead I walked under the grey-black sky, past trashed houses with graffiti on them and closed-down shops all boarded up. While I walked I tried to get a grip, but the black hole was like something I'd forgotten. It was a pain to do with Blazing Star. Something that made us proper blood brothers.

I ended up in a scruffy car park with bashed-out lights and clouds coming over.

And that's when I heard these footsteps clumping, coming over to where I was. When I walked faster, so did the steps, and I remembered what I'd seen on TV with folks getting mugged and beaten up while people at home were just eating their tea and saying, 'Well, fancy being there anyway.'

I started to run and I was right near the road with the chance of some people and cars going past, when this hand came down and gripped my shoulder and terror made me freeze to the spot.

Dancing with Michelle

'You stupid bogger! What you running for?'

Michelle's voice came out of the dark and I half turned round to look at her, but she'd still got my shoulder clutched in her hand like she was trying her best to hold me down.

'Why d'you think?' I shouted back in this voice that sounded too thin and scared.

'You thought I was going to mug you, right? Well, thanks a bunch, I'm dead flattered.'

After she'd said that Michelle took her hand away and we both stood there breathless and staring under the stupid lights. Michelle had her black leather jacket on again, and maybe it was the damp in the air but her bright red spikes had started to droop and she looked like a bedraggled, scruffy hen.

I started to laugh, mainly from nerves, and Michelle looked at me suspiciously. 'What you laughing at, anyway?'

'Nothing much. Just you,' I said.

And she sniffed and wiped her nose on her sleeve and said, 'Yeah. Well. It'd be nice if you let me in on the joke.'

When she finished speaking we both relaxed. Michelle leaned against a lamppost and gave a cough, then pulled a packet of fags from her pocket.

'Want one?' she asked me, very politely. 'Oh no. Sorry. I forgot. You don't.'

I watched her put the fag in her mouth and light it and slowly blow the smoke out. In the light from the lamp her face looked green with big black sockets instead of eyes.

'What are you doing round here?' I said in the end.

Michelle wafted the smoke away from her face with a hand full of glinting silver rings. 'I live up there. With me auntie and mum. They're out, mostly. I look after myself.'

'Yeah, right.'

'And what're *you* doing here?'

'Been out to Sutton to look at the stars. Got dropped here. Now I'm just off home.'

'Stars? What stars?' Michelle said, and coughed again with a hand to her mouth.

'You want to give them up,' I said. 'Leonides. That's what I went to look at tonight.'

'And who's this Leo then, when he's at home?'

'He's a meteor. You see him best at this time of year. There's hundreds of stars just shooting about. It's like bonfire night with knobs on, right? Look, if you try real hard you can see a few of them shooting about just over there.'

Michelle moved her shoulders from off the lamppost. You could hear her leather jacket creaking and the black puddles where her eyes should be glinted a moment and then went dark.

'So where are they, then? You having me on?'

'Put your fag out and come over here.'

With a sigh Michelle dropped her fag to the ground and stamped it out with her great heavy boot. She came up to stand where the lights had blown and I pointed the stars out, shooting the sky like tiny tracers playing games, backwards and forwards across the sky.

'Blimey,' she said. I could smell cigarettes. 'I mean, strewth. Bogger me. Who'd have thought?'

She craned her neck with her hands to her eyes curled up like binoculars. 'Are they real or what? I mean, how about that! I mean, folks go to the pub and the flicks and that and this is what's going on outside!'

'There's usually something at this time of year. You just have to know what to look for when.'

'Right. Yeah. They're getting fainter now.'

'We'd best be getting off home again.'

'Hang on a sec.' Michelle creaked her arms back to her sides then stuck her hands in two narrow pockets slanting down in front of her ribs. The jacket ballooned out behind her and Michelle's blobby face turned round.

'I don't need to go back home just yet. No one'll miss me.' She shrugged and kicked. 'Maybe we could do that dancing now. You know – the stuff you reckon you do with your gran.'

'You what?' I said, with my jaw dropped down.

'*Dancing*! You know! Like you do with your gran!'

'We can't do that! It's dark and it's late! And anyway, we haven't got any music. How'd we be able to dance without?'

'You could hum,' Michelle said. She sounded deflated, and even with her Doc Martens on she looked smaller than usual, and scraggier. I was staring at her and chewing my lip and you could hear cars chugging by on the road in the distance. It was cold and I definitely didn't want to dance.

'We could have a go at a waltz,' I said.

'Yeah! Right! Great! You're on!'

She took her hands out of her pockets and just stood there looking, and I twigged I'd have to take hold of her hand. I'd have to put my arm round her leather waist, and this was Michelle, the tough kid in class!

'Well, go on then,' she said. 'What do I do? I can't just stand here like a nerd all night.'

'You have to put your right hand in my left hand. And then my other arm goes round your waist and then you walk backwards on your left leg, then you step to one side and do the same with your right.'

Michelle put her bony hand in mine and clumped a step

back, giggling and sniffing and clanking the chains she had on her jeans.

'Step to your left,' I said, sounding like Gran and trying to move her with the arm on her waist.

She moved the wrong way and stepped on my toe and I stopped and said, 'Stop mucking about. When I say left leg I don't mean right. And that was my toe you just stepped on.'

'Yeah. Okey-dokey. Keep your cool. Blimey, Geoffrey, it's worse than school.'

After that we had another go, and Michelle stepped back and moved to the left so my leg followed hers and we got it right.

'Good,' I said. 'Now you know how it's done. We can push off home and get warmed up.'

'S'ppose.' Michelle gave another creaking shrug and fixed her dark sockets on the ground. Then this car gave a hoot and she looked up and said, 'We could try it with music. What d'you say? You could hum something, or sing if you want. It'd help me like, to get it right.'

So that's when I started humming *They Try to Tell Us We're Too Young* which wasn't exactly the right sort of beat but was all I could think of in the dark right then. Michelle was hanging off my arm, clumping about with her chains jangling and the spikes of her hair getting up my nose. And there was still this weird yellow light and the empty houses and the gutted shops.

In a while Michelle started singing out loud, or bawling more like, at the top of her voice. And in a minute or so I stopped my hum and started to sing along with her, so we were both of us clumping about in this waltz and yelling out loud at the same time, *'They try to tell us we're to young, la-laaa la-la-la-la-la-laaa'* mostly because we didn't know the words.

Then it started to rain. Without warning clouds came over and the yellow lights dimmed and rain was drumming off Michelle's leather jacket and pounding off my anorak.

'Bogger! Bogger!' Michelle yelled. 'I was just starting to enjoy myself! Oy, Geoffrey! We better run!'

We ran to a tree where the road began and I said, 'Right. I'd better be getting off home.'

A car swished past, its wipers going and headlights glaring like two bright eyes. In the light of them I saw Michelle's face with black stuff running in lines down it.

She said, 'Yeah. Right,' and started to run, then stopped and turned and yelled at me, 'You see Darren? I did that! I told you he was a dick-head right?' She fetched a hand out from under her jacket and rubbed her silver rings on her chest. Then she turned round and started running again, and I waited a second and did the same.

When I got home Gran said, 'You're wet. Go and get out of those clothes, Geoffrey, then come and sit down in front of the fire.'

I did what she said and Gran brought me a drink and smoothed my wet hair with her freckled hand. She said, 'You do take after your mother, you know. She always seemed to be out in the cold. She liked looking at things the same as you. But there . . .'

Gran gazed at the fire and closed her mouth and I thought of Mum laughing with her hair windswept when we'd been for a walk up Ravenscar. The sun was shining and you could hear the sea. Gulls were wheeling and screaming out and Dad was saying, 'That's a kittiwake. They say they're the souls of long-lost children.' And Mum squeezed my arm and pulled my hair and said, 'Well, Geoffrey, we'd better hang on to you.'

I could still see their faces when I got into bed. They were clear as clear, as if they'd never left. As if Africa had somehow dropped off the map and everything was like it should have been.

Later I slept and started to dream. I saw this black thing in the sky, a long way off but coming my way. Was it the hawk or was it the horse? I never found out because I woke up then and looked at my clock in the gloomy dawn. It was six o'clock on Saturday morning. I lay back down and closed my eyes and tried to switch the dream back on. But I couldn't because in another twelve hours I'd be getting myself all dressed up and spruce, ready to dance on Gala Night.

Blood Brothers

Gran kept me busy all next day.

'I'm having my hair done at Betty's this morning, so you'll have to do the shopping, Geoffrey. And you might try flicking a duster round. Oh, and pop round to Ivy's with these magazines.'

The magazines all had people with grey hair on the front and headlines like, 'I Wrote My First Book at Seventy-four!'

I went round to Ivy's and banged at the door and after a while the chain rattled and Ivy's face came round the gap. 'Geoffrey!' she said. 'This is a surprise! Come in me duck, while I get sorted out.'

Ivy still had rollers stuck in her hair and the radio was tuned to Radio 2 with this schmaltzy music playing really loud.

I said, 'I've only come to bring you these.'

'Well now.' Ivy was looking flustered. 'It's not often I

have a young man here. And I've got something for you, Geoffrey, my duck. Hang on while I go and fetch it down.'

Ivy disappeared up the narrow box-stairs and I sat on a lumpy velvet chair and looked at a picture on the wall. The picture showed a thin young woman, all done up in a long white dress with a veil coming down nearly over her eyes. She was holding on to the arm of a man and both of them were smiling these weird, stiff, smiles. Next to it there was another photo showing Ivy with a wavy perm and a dress with lots off frills and sequins, dancing with the same man in a dickie bow.

'Here we are.' Ivy came back down. The curlers were gone from out of her hair and she'd lipstick on, and some face powder. 'I thought you'd like it for tonight, my duck. It was my Stan's and it brought us luck. Open it, love, and have a look.'

A tissue-paper parcel was put in my hands and Ivy stepped back with this look on her face, sort of pleased and excited, like she could hardly wait.

I opened the parcel and gave a gasp, only not with pleasure like Ivy thought, but because what she gave me was so gross.

Inside the paper was this dickie bow. The same one Stan wore in the photograph. It was blue with red spots on and attached to elastic that went round under your turned-down collar so only the dickie showed at the front.

'Thanks,' I said, trying not to sound glum.

And Ivy beamed and touched the dickie and said, 'I shall think of Stan now when I look at you.'

I went off after that with Gran's shopping list and the dickie carefully wrapped again and put in my pocket by Ivy, saying, 'There now. You want to keep that safe. I shall see you tonight in it, Geoffrey. Tarra!'

Gran's list said oranges and coal-tar soap, so I went to the greengrocer's and then to Boots, and when I came outside again I stood in the street and tried not to think about Blazing Star.

I'd woken up again later that morning thinking about him, like he was a part of me that I couldn't ever switch off, and I knew that something bad had happened to him. I knew it as soon as the star disappeared, as soon as I got the pain in my chest and saw the black hole in the sky. And we were blood brothers, me and Blazing star. Blood brothers for ever under the skin, so whatever bad thing had happened to him would somehow happen to me as well.

I didn't go round to Hockley Lane because I was afraid to. I went to the Co-op and the library instead. When I'd done the shopping I went straight home and Gran was back looking very smart. Her hair was set in waves and curls and even though I thought she looked better before, I said, 'Your hair looks nice, Gran.'

And Gran patted it and twiddled a curl and said, 'Betty knows what she's about.'

After that I showed her the dickie bow. 'It's horrible!' I said. 'I can't wear that!. Can we pretend we've lost it, Gran? Maybe she won't notice if I don't have it on.'

'Of course she'll notice!' Gran said, shocked. 'I grant you we might not have chosen it, but it was kindly meant, love, remember that. And sometimes we have to do things we don't want, or risk an upset and it's not worth that. You'll be wearing that dickie tonight, Geoffrey, so you'd better start thinking along those lines.'

For the rest of the day I helped Gran with the chores. Then later I went upstairs to get ready and she came in with the dickie bow. After she fixed it round my neck I looked at myself in the mirror again and I didn't look magnificent like Blazing Star, I reckoned I looked like a circus dog, and the shirt would have looked good on a girl.

But Gran was excited, her cheeks were flushed and she'd a dress on I hadn't seen before. 'Well,' she said, 'it's not really new, but I know who it's come from, that's the main thing.'

The dress was blue in silky stuff with little flowers going down the front. Gran had shoes to match and a blue hand-bag. She said, 'It's a pity I've got to wear that old coat, but I'll take it off quick when we get inside.'

We set off arm-in-arm with Gran's shoes in a bag and you could see other ladies coming out of their houses with bags in their hands and their best coats on.

At the hotel there was a man on the door wearing a fancy uniform. He said, 'Could you have your tickets ready, ladies, please? Thank you so much. There are drinks over there, so help yourselves, then pass straight through to the Grand Ballroom.'

We went in a room with this great net up and you could see it bulging with red balloons. To begin with people chatted and drank and said stuff like, 'That colour suits you. You should wear it more often. Have you seen Marjorie's new red dress?' And, 'Of course, we don't expect to win. The spot prize could go to anyone.' In the background a band was playing slow tunes with the men all done up in white bow ties, and you could hear the waitresses chuntering on and stuff being clanked about in the kitchen.

When we'd chatted enough this voice shouted out, 'Lad*ees* and Gentle*men*! Please take your seats. Dinner will be served in five minutes' time.'

We sat at a table with Ivy and Vera, and Ivy said, 'You look real smart in that dickie bow, Geoffrey. It takes me back, that it does, seeing it on you tonight.' Then she took out a hanky and blew her nose and Vera said, 'Well, you're the only bloke we've got over here. I reckon you'll be busy tonight, Geoffrey.'

The dinner was better than even Gran had said. There was prawn cocktail just to start, and then some soup, and then some pork done up in a sauce. Pudding was trifle or apple pie and when we'd had the coffee and chocolates this voice came again.

'Lad*ees* and gentle*men*! The band will now play a swing-time tune. So take your partners for the first dance!'

Gran gave a gasp and sat up straight and dug me dead sharp in the ribs and said, 'Come on, Geoffrey! You could dance this one. It'll get us both warmed up a bit, like.'

Gran and I danced in this great big circle with everyone doing stuff at the same time, and when we got near the band a bloke gave us a wink and Gran said, 'I reckon he's spotted my new dress.'

After the swing it was a cha-cha-cha, and Ivy said, with her eyes on my shirt, 'I used to love dancing this with Stan.'

Then Gran gave me a nudge and I said to Ivy, 'Would you like to dance?'

And Ivy said, 'I'd love to, thank you, Geoffrey, my dear.'

So I cha-cha-ed with Ivy and when we got to the band the man gave us another wink and Ivy said, 'I think he likes my new hair-do.'

For the next half-hour I never sat down because ladies kept coming up to Gran. They said, 'Won't you introduce us to this young man?' And, 'He's a fine young chap, that he is, to be sure.'

So I sauntered and quick-stepped and did a slow fox-trot while the ladies said how brilliant I was. They said I reminded them of Fred or George and they hoped as how I'd come again and maybe we could do a Military Two-step or a Valeta or the Monet Waltz.

I was getting flushed and enjoying myself, what with the trifle and the music and the dance. Then Gran said, 'You'd better make sure you save some puff. It'll be the Caribbean Foxtrot any time now, and I reckon we'll dance 'em into the ground.'

After that there was a Ladies' Excuse Me Waltz and three ladies came over at the same time and Gran said, 'I'd better draw a line on the floor, Geoffrey. I can see you're that much in demand!'

The music finished and there was a gap before a man came up to the microphone. He said, 'Lad*ees* and gentle*men*! The time has come for tonight's spot prize! The winners will take home chocolates and wine and their photo will be in *The Evening Post*. So will you take your partners now, one and all for the Caribbean Foxtrot – let's take it away!'

A few people clapped then, and this music began and Gran took my hand and we went on to the floor. We started to dance to *Unforgettable* and for once Gran didn't tell me what to do. Instead she danced with her eyes shut tight and suddenly it was like stuff came together, not just the steps she'd taught me at home, or the other people gliding round, but the magic I felt on that first afternoon.

In the middle of the dance this spotlight came on. It went

swooping and dipping right round the room, lighting up one couple and then another. Couples smiled when the light was on them and put a bit more pep in their dance. Then the spotlight came to rest on us, and Gran blinked a bit and opened her eyes. She said, 'Well now, Geoffrey, you're doing great. Just enjoy yourself, love, that's the thing.'

After that the music changed to *They Try to Tell Us We're Too Young* and the spotlight went from white to red and some people gasped and looked excited. A little ripple went round the room. Somebody said, 'This is it, then.' The light stayed on a couple I didn't know, and folks looked at them and then glanced away before the beam switched to someone else. It stayed on the next couple a minute or two, then went back to the first and stayed on them. I heard someone say, 'They must have won,' and another ripple went right round the room while folks carried on dancing and trying to smile.

I was pretending not to be disappointed, but fretting about what Gran might think, when all at once the spotlight moved. It swooped again and hovered a bit before it made its mind up and landed on us. We carried on dancing like we hadn't noticed, and turned and feathered and did a three-step. After that the light flickered and looked unsure, and the first couple were smiling like they'd already won.

Gran said very softly in my ear, 'This doesn't matter at all, Geoffrey. The main thing is, we've enjoyed the dance.'

Then suddenly the light came back. It stayed on us while

we dipped and turned. It changed from white to red and gold. After that this voice came booming out.

'Lad*ees* and gentle*men*! The winner of tonight's spot prize is the lady in the flowered blue dress partnered by the tall young man! So will you put your hands together for the winning couple! And very well done to both of you! Thanks to the rest for being such sports!'

The dancing stopped for a while after that and everyone clapped and looked at us. We had to go on the stage and collect our prizes and the man in the band winked at us again. After that we danced round the room on our own with folks looking and clapping when we went past, and Gran beaming at them and nodding her head.

Gran said later, 'You go and dance with Ivy, love. I need a chance to get me puff back, and me corn's starting to play up again.'

So I danced with Ivy and then with Hilda and everything would have been just great; but suddenly it was eleven o'clock. I was dancing with Hilda when these balloons came down. The net overhead opened silently and to begin with they floated down a few at a time and I stopped and looked up like everyone else.

And that's when this change happened suddenly. I was watching the balloons that were a round, bright red, when all at once they stopped being balloons and turned instead into drops of blood. The blood was dropping down and down until you couldn't see anything except the blood and people behind it fading away.

After that there was no sound in the room. My mouth was open to make a scream that didn't come, and in the silence I knew Blazing Star was there. He was a blood-red light on the pink plush chairs and tables littered with streamers and wine. The blood falling sounded like drums beating and I knew Blazing Star had come for me and would keep on coming until I went back to him.

Then suddenly he disappeared. A light went off in my head and the blood stopped being a drum and became just balloons with people catching them while I stood there with tears welling up in my eyes.

I pulled a hanky out of my pocket and pretended I was blowing my nose. Gran said, 'You all right, love? You look a bit pale.'

'I'm OK. It's just the heat.'

The band started playing *When I Grow Too Old to Dream* and Gran said, 'Come on, Geoffrey, we'll get our coats.'

Gran took my arm and we walked home slowly and we'd nearly got there when she said, 'What's that star that's following us? I don't think I've seen the like before.'

Without even looking I knew what it was. You could see the glow from it like a path in front, waiting for me to go down it.

'Dunno,' I said.

'Well,' Gran paused and looked at me, 'I expect you'll find out eventually.'

When we got home I went to bed but the star was still there, hovering. You could see the light from it through the curtains and I knew Blazing Star was waiting for me to finish my journey, and I had to go and find him. Soon.

The Truth

Gran said at breakfast, 'We'll give those chocolates to Ivy, Geoffrey. She deserves them for being so kind to you. You could take 'em round to her later on.'

'Eh?' I said, and Gran looked impatient. 'You're wool-gathering, Geoffrey. You were up too late. I said you can take them chocs round to Ivy later. Now, have you finished eating, or do you want some more?'

When I didn't reply she looked even crosser and clashed the breakfast dishes about. After breakfast I went up to my room and I could hear the drums again from last night. They were playing this weird, syncopated beat, not so much Native American like you hear in films, but more like a kind of African beat that got louder and louder and ended up with a crash, as if the drum-sticks had been thrown down suddenly.

When the beat finished I went to a drawer and got out a photo of Mum and Dad. It was hot and they were both wearing white sun hats and the hats put a shadow over their faces. We'd been on a picnic and we'd been watching birds. We were watching a lapwing stalking about and we admired the crest and its tumbling *kie-wit*. Then Dad said suddenly, 'That's a hawk hovering about up there. This is a funny place for it. Look – you can see it floating over that tree. It must be an old bird because it's so dark.'

I looked up and saw the hawk circling and coming nearer to us. In a minute it was right over our heads and its colour had changed from brown to black and it was slowly starting its long swoop down.

'NO!' I shouted out loud now. 'Hop it, will you? Just go away!'

To make it go I got up and went out. I took the chocolates and the bow tie round to Ivy and she came to the door in her dressing-gown.

'Oh, Geoffrey, love,' she said, beaming, 'I can't ask you in. But thank your gran, will you, for this kind thought? You did well last night, Geoffrey, to win that prize. My Stan's tie must have brought you luck. I expect your gran's real proud of you.'

When I'd been to Ivy's I went down Hockley and mooched up the street where the factory was. There was no one around. The factory looked ordinary and I went back home and hung about, scowling and feeling fed up.

For the rest of the day I got on Gran's nerves. 'What's the matter with you today, Geoffrey? You're just like a blinking cat on hot bricks. Why don't you do your stamp album?'

Only nothing she suggested made me settle down and I went up to bed feeling irritable.

The next day it was dark and wet. Clouds were swirling over Green's Mill. Leaves were being dashed off the trees and you could hear thunder cracking over Trent Bridge.

At school nobody said anything much. Even Darren just crossed his eyes and make a rude sign with his hand. Peter Bryant asked me to neet him at four. 'We could go down town and just chill out. You know – look at girls and have a fag and that.'

'No, ta,' I said. 'It's not my scene.' And Peter looked offended and nearly mouthed off, but changed his mind and walked away.

At four o'clock I was going down Hockley but never made it to Star Knitwear. I was thinking about Blazing Star when there was this sudden flash of something in my head and Blazing Star appeared in it like a dazzle of lightning and was still there when it died away.

He was sitting on a horse I didn't know and dawn was coming up behind him. When he saw me he got off the horse that was all painted up with moons and stars. A huge star was painted on his chest that was silver with a bright red eye, and the eye seemed to look directly at you and follow you round wherever you went.

On the ground Blazing Star looked bigger again. His skin was stretched across his face and there were lines running down from his nose to his mouth so he looked like he was an old-young man. On his face there were stripes in bright blood red and a blood-red parting went down his hair. Round his waist he wore the cloth thing again and his body was painted with circles like eyes.

But his own eyes were still and bleak and unsmiling. You could hear his horse jangle and champ at the bit but Blazing Star never said anything. He just looked in silence while the wind reared up and ruffled the tall feathers on his head.

The silence between us was a thing you could touch, but at last I saw his lips start to move.

'Today I kill a man, Magic Eyes.' There was a spear in his right hand that glinted red. On his thigh was a painting like a skeleton.

'Why?' I asked, and looked at the ground with little flowers on it like normal earth.

'I must avenge my beloved father today.'

'What happened to him?' I asked, choked up, because I saw his father's hand come out and go over Long Horn's very gently, that first day when we broke the horse.

'He fell at the hands of a Cree, Magic Eyes. I go today to honour his name.'

'My name's not Magic Eyes, it's Geoffrey,' I said. 'Why can't you just pray for him?'

When I said that Blazing Star came closer. By then the sun was starting to show and instead of making things brighter and clearer, it made me believe time had nearly run out.

'I prayed for *you*, Gee-ooff,' he said.

And I reckon his shadow was over me then because when I looked up it seemed darker somehow. Blazing Star's eyes were still black and unsmiling, but I thought I saw a sadness in them, so deep I had to look away.

'Well,' I said, and shrugged and looked down and tried not to cry in front of him.

After that his left hand came on to my shoulder so I could feel the weight of it, and the heat. He said very softly, 'I prayed because I am afraid, Gee-ooff. I have never harmed a man before.'

I gave a sniff and wiped my eyes. 'You're never afraid!' I yelled at him. 'You can't be! I rely on you! If you're afraid, then I will be, because you're who I get my courage from!'

When I finished yelling the sun gave a lurch and came up higher suddenly. Blazing Star's hand stayed where it was.

'What are you afraid of, Gee-ooff?' he asked.

And a sigh came out that I couldn't stop. Of everything, I wanted to say. Of being different and not fitting in. Of always being the butt of jokes. Of not having a proper friend.

I stared down at the flowers and then looked up. Very clearly and slowly I said to him, 'I'm afraid that Mum and

Dad are dead, and I never believed it up until now.'

Blazing Star stood quiet and still and just looked at me sternly like he already knew. Then he took his hand away from my shoulder and sprang very lightly on to his horse. The horse tossed its mane and champed the bit and did a side-step on its delicate feet. I put a hand out on to its nose. Without looking at Blazing Star I said, 'Good luck, my friend. May you live to see another day.'

And Blazing Star leaned from his painted saddle so a black wing of hair fell over his face. He put his strong hand over mine. 'Being afraid is not important, Gee-ooff. Fearless people are not brave. It is what you do that the Gods will judge.'

After that he sat up straight and proud and the sun flared out in a dazzling ray. It lit up Blazing Star's shiny hair and the stripes and swirls going over his face. His eyes gave off sparks like red lights flashing and his spear was raised up in a gleaming salute.

He wheeled his horse round and I shouted, scared, 'I'll see you again won't I, very soon?'

Blazing Star dug his heels into the horse and shouted back to me over his shoulder, 'In your dreams, Magic Eyes! You will see me there!'

The next thing that happened, happened fast. Blazing Star was beginning to thunder away. You could see his hair flying back in the sun and I think he shouted something else, like, 'Go now, and the Powers be always with you, my friend!' At the same time as this horse appeared. It was my horse, the black one we stole in the raid, suddenly rearing in front of me, so I was picked up and flown off like the wind. Faster and faster we went down the Plain and I could see Blazing Star with his spear raised up; I could see us both doing the dawn raid; I could see the buffalo hunt and the hard winter, and Long Horn laughing when he broke in the horse, and shooting arrows with his friends.

When the whirling stopped the horse was just a dark shape in my head. I blinked to clear it and the indian was there on the street in front of me. His spear was raised in a shining flash. His eyes sparked red, his teeth flashed white; his skin was dazzling with stars and moons. He looked brilliant, magnificent. Like a blazing star.

But suddenly a light went out. The dazzle didn't fade, it was just switched off and I walked back to Gran's with my shoulders hunched. The rain had stopped and the sky was clearing. You could see Jupiter glowing like a small white fire, but there was no sign anywhere of Blazing Star. When I got in the house I said to Gran, 'I feel a bit knackered. I'm going to bed.'

'Don't you want your cocoa?' Gran sounded worried.

'Nah. I just want to get my head down now.'

I got into bed and my head seemed to hurt and I felt Blazing Star's hand on my shoulder again. In my ear his voice came clear as clear, *'Being afraid is not important . . . it is what you do that the Gods will judge . . .'*

I woke up in the morning feeling calm and the feeling stayed with me all day long, even though I'd admitted the truth; that Mum and Dad hadn't left me deliberately. They'd both been killed in a plane crash. They'd been going to Africa for just one week to try and sort out some work of Dad's when their plane went down in a stupid desert and all the passengers were killed.

I didn't let on to Gran I knew. I wanted to look at what had happened first like you see it in a newspaper or on the telly. PLANE GOES DOWN. NO SURVIVORS. I thought I might get used to it faster if I pictured it in black and white.

At breakfast Gran looked worriedly at me. 'Are you all right, Geoffrey?' she asked. 'You looked a bit peaky to me last night.'

'I'm fine, Gran. Honest. And call me Geoff. I like it better, it suits me more. And anyway, no one's ever called Geoffrey these days.'

'It's the name your mum and dad gave you and I've never thought it was right cut short. What's wrong with Geoffrey all of a sudden? I knew there was something odd going on.'

Gran stopped looking worried and looked cross instead and I got up and put my arms round her waist.

'I'm just growing up, Gran,' I said.

Gran gave a sniff and pushed me off and ran some water into a bowl. She said, 'Yes. Well. I suppose you are. I'm still trying my best to get used to it.'

Later on I went to school, still full of this calm feeling, and some kids in English were showing off while Miss Turner looked helpless and twittered at them. We were doing about doubling and I was reading the wall with this chart on it that said,

> *REBEL – REBELLING*
> *QUARREL – QUARRELLING*

which seemed to me to be kind of apt. But then suddenly I got fed up and turned round to Darren and the other kids and said, 'Shut up, will you? I'm trying to work.'

I saw Michelle look over at me. She put a hand up to her chest and rubbed her silver rings on it. Next thing is some kid shouts out, 'Shut up yourself, chunk,' and then went very quiet and swallowed hard and muttered, 'No offence.'

When we had a break Michelle came up. She looked cold under her leather jacket. Her face was pinched and she'd got no gloves.

'Hey-up, Geoffrey,' she said, and huffed on her hands. 'Want to meet me later today? We could do some more dancing if you like. It's dead cool, that is. We could go to your gran's.'

'Oh yeah?' I said to her, dead cool back. 'I'm called Geoff now, by the way. And another thing while I think about it – have you been warning the other kids off?'

'Might have been,' she said, and shrugged. 'I just think you're different. You know – kind of weird – only not weird *weird*. I mean, you go your own way.'

'Fine,' I said, 'and you can go yours. And don't go fighting any battles for me. I can sort myself out, thanks very much.'

'Right,' she said. And stayed where she was and stamped her big boots on the ground. When a kid came up she sent them away. 'I'm busy,' she said, 'I'll see you again.' Then she folded her arms across her chest and blew a grey bubble on her gum and said, 'You don't care, do you? I mean, you *don't*.'

And that's when I gave this great big sigh and looked at the sky with a fat rain cloud. In front of us kids were loafing about looking bored and fed up and at a loose end. Then a shaft of light came bursting out and I remembered Blazing Star on the Plain. *It's what you do that the Gods will judge . . .*

'Are your folks out all the time?' I asked.

'Mostly,' Michelle shrugged again. 'I don't care. They do what they want.'

'I might be free tomorrow,' I said. 'You could come up to Gran's when you've had your tea. I reckon she could show you how best to dance.'

'OK.' Michelle yawned and slouched away. Then she

stopped suddenly and looked back and said, 'Why Geoff? I mean, why now? What *for*?

'Just seems like a good idea,' I said.

'Yeah. Right. So long then.'

'See you around – oh, and Michelle. I care about all sorts of stuff. Just not the same stuff as Darren and Shane.'

She gave me wave and wandered off and later I went home to Gran.

Gran was drinking tea. When I came in she said, 'There's some in the pot. I've only just made it, Geoffrey – Geoff.'

I poured the tea out and went to sit down. Then I took a few sips of it and said, 'Mum and Dad named me Geoffrey, Gran. But they're dead now, aren't they? So calling me Geoff won't hurt them.'

Gran's cup made a rattle when it went on the saucer, and she took her feet off the patchwork pouffe.

'I never thought you believed it,' she said. 'I thought you'd somehow cut it off. It's worried me these last few months. Are you all right, Geoff? I mean, now you've said . . . they loved you, you know, more than anyone else. They wouldn't want you to be miserable.'

'I'm all right now. I just took my time. And anyway, I've had some help . . .'

'Who from?' said Gran, indignantly.

'Just a friend,' I said. 'No one you know. I won't see them again. I don't need to.'

'Is it a girlfriend?' Gran asked me, suddenly sharp.

'No!' I said. 'But it could be, soon!'

I laughed and thought of Michelle's great boots dodging the sofa and the glass cabinet where Gran kept her best bits of china on show.

'I've a friend coming tomorrow,' I said. 'She's called Michelle. She wants to meet you. She thinks you can teach her how to dance.'

'Oh, does she now?' Gran sounded pleased. 'She could come for tea if you want, Geoffre – Geoff.'

'Thanks,' I said. 'I'll ask her, Gran.'

After supper I went to my room and looked at myself in the speckly mirror. I thought I might get a new hairstyle, kind of stiff and spiky. I might grow sideburns. And if Gran could afford it I'd get some black jeans with a leather belt that went through the loops, and a black leather jacket from the Oxfam shop.

After that I went to lie on the bed, and I took out some photos of Mum and Dad. Only not the ones in the photograph album, they were just pictures like anyone took. The photos I looked at were in my head, all in glorious technicolour. I could see Africa dead bright and clear. I could see Mum and Dad like they always were and always would be when I wanted them.

But I could never see the indian. Instead there was just this single star whirring in the black night sky. There were sparks trailing off it, it had a bright red eye and no one else could see it but me.